Cold Country

JD Salyers

Published by Pinwheel Books, 2018.

This is a work of fiction. Similarities to real people, places, or events are entirely coincidental.

COLD COUNTRY

First edition. March 11, 2018.

Copyright © 2018 JD Salyers.

Written by JD Salyers.

Cold Country

Chapter One

Abel Welch walked along the riverbank, watching dead leaves swirl like blood in the fast moving water. The snowmelt was down to a trickle now, but it would start all over when the storm hit tonight. There wouldn't be too much snow - when he was a boy he remembered snow drifts as tall as his head. These days they were lucky to get a foot, lucky to get six inches some years.

Still, the news this morning said that this one might be the storm of the century, and they called for up to twenty-four inches. Not that they knew what they were talking about most of the time. But fat grey clouds were scudding across the sky and the wind had a bite to it, so maybe they weren't so wrong. The afternoon would tell.

He scanned the water with his eyes, grinning a little when he caught sight of Rick Fuller's pale dead body, bobbing farther downstream. As he watched, the body sank out of sight, then heaved up, splashing and spinning as it smacked against a boulder. It was pure lucky that Rick was dressed in dark clothes when Abel killed him, now, wasn't it? With any luck, Rick would hit the bend in the river at speed and get twisted up in the brush that hung out over the water. There he'd stay until at least spring, because nobody came down this section of the river, not this time of year.

The only people around lived in the place behind him, a beat-to-hell double wide house trailer where Rick lived - used to live - with his nurse wife Patty and their three maggots. Abel's stay was supposed to be temporary, and he assumed that now Rick was gone, it would be. Or maybe Patty would pack up the kids and head to her momma's over in Summersville. Maybe he would offer to keep house for her until she decided what to do with the place.

As long as the kids didn't run up on their dead daddy while they were playing outside. Kids saw everything.

Rick's soggy body dipped out of sight again, under the fast moving current. Abel called it good enough and turned to go into the house, favoring his knee as he climbed the bank.

The cold seemed colder these days. It set his bones to aching in ways that made him want to crawl back to bed and stay there 'til March.

Of course, that might just be him, getting older.

His work history pointed that way, anyway. His laboring days were mostly over, except for odd jobs he picked up here and there. Lately, he tried not to do anything more strenuous than traveling to the bank once a month and withdrawing his disability allowance. He didn't like not being able to hold it in his hands.

His disability was a bad back and twinges in his knees. The twinges came from the last time he fell off a ladder. He'd been trying to replace a few shingles on the three-story auction barn that day, the one down in Randolph. Something spooked him, probably one of the bats that lived up there. He never saw what it was, just a dark shape that broke through one of the upper air vents and brushed his face. He swiped at it, which turned out to be a mistake. He'd half fallen, just enough to land wrong on the rungs and twist something out of whack

The bad back was from thirty years of fighting livestock at that same auction house. Damned bulls were just big furry boulders, falling and trampling everything to get to a safety they would never find. The cows, too, and they were all too dumb to know it. By the time he got quit of that place, he hated animals.

They didn't like him much, either. Part of his job, back then, was to take the sick and damaged animals out back of the auction house and shoot them in the head. Abel recognized the wary hatred in those dull, dark eyes whenever he'd do that. Afterward, he'd use the forklift to tip them over the cliff into the hollow below. That way they were out of the sight of the buyers or any inspectors that happened to be nosing around. If there was an animal hell, he figured he would get there one of these days. It was a steady job, but he was glad to be quit of it.

At the top of the bank he paused to try kicking some of the mud off his boot soles, but most of it held, even when he stomped. He walked over to the rickety back steps and kicked harder, hurting his toe bad enough to cuss, but at least his boots were cleaner. Up here on the flat, away from the water, mud was only an inch deep, instead of three.

Once he dreamed all those cows came back, trudging up out of that dark deep hole, strips of rotting hide and beef falling off their useless hocks. He could see the white stretch of tendons and the black red of dried blood where muscle once layered their bones. They were coming for him, in the dream, and every single one of 'em had a bold black hole between their eyes. Like the barrel of a gun or one of them laser beams, finding him out and coming ever his way.

His Pap would have called him stupid, and this time at least, he would have been right. Abel didn't consider himself stupid, but dreams like that made him wonder if there was some odd thing in his brain. Mayhap there was, and maybe one day the odd thing would catch up with him like it had his own Pap, but it hadn't happened yet.

Right now he was content to stay with the Fullers, who were half his age and dumber than most of those cows he'd put down. Of course, his stay with the river family was about to end, wasn't it? Sometime later today, a few hours from now, most likely. Around the time Patty got home from work and realized Rick was gone.

He smiled at the water below his soppy Workman Barnbusters. The laces were loose, so the mud threatened to suck them off his feet with every step, but he still didn't bother tying them. He'd been wearing them for nearly six years, and they weren't too broke, except for the waterproofing wearing off and one heel trying to split loose from the leather. It wasn't ten years ago he would have worn through a pair every season, but those days were past, if he had anything to say about it.

His only problem - well, besides the Fuller problem that would deal a hand later - was that the disability didn't quite stretch as far as he needed. The politicians promised more every election season, but he weren't holding his breath over that. Even with the kindness of the Fullers and the free food he picked up at the gimmee store, he needed folding money. For Beam and cigarettes, mostly. Patty Fuller, that nosy bitch, had told him his money would last a hell of a lot longer if he'd give 'em up, but she didn't understand. The Beam was for the pain, the smokes - and pot when he could get it - was for his nerves.

It wasn't like he had health insurance. It wasn't like he worked at the hospital like her, either. He could have. Patty had brought home applications a couple of times, saying they were in dire need of *custodians*, like that word meant something fancier than trash man. He might have done it, too, but every time he thought about it, a giant, solid wall rose up in his mind. It towered over every other thing that had ever happened to him, good or bad. It was a thick wall, too, one he couldn't see over and one he'd never be able to climb. When it rose up, he was just stopped dead in his Barnbusters, unable to take the next step. It was worrying, probably something he needed to see the doctor about. A...what were they called? A mental health specialist, which sounded to him like a fancy way to say trash man. A mental trash man, you could say.

He grinned at that and fished two fingers into his coat pocket, pulling out a Marlboro from the softpack. He put it in his mouth and dug in again for the lighter. The smoke burned his throat and he liked that. He threw back his head and stared at the clouds again.

Off somewhere on the mountain, he heard a few yips from a pack of coyotes that'd been hanging around lately. He looked up toward the peak, where it loomed black against the sky, and for a few moments he wished he still had his guns. Even a single one of his handguns would come in handy at times, living out here. It would have come in handy this morning, for sure. He grinned harder, raised a finger gun toward the tree line and pretended to blow a coyote away.

Of course, Patty Fuller would never have let him live here if he'd owned arms. It was the first thing she asked him six months ago, when he'd come home with Rick from the Big Sip. Was he armed, and did he have a job?

Damned woman questions. He'd told her the truth - no to both - and she told Rick he could stay. For a while. That was one of those tricky phrases that women used to keep control of the rules, now, wasn't it?

For a while. *Until I change my mind,* she meant, and they all three knew it, standing there in her fancy double wide kitchen with the dishwasher and the fridge that had two doors and smudged glass shelves. If he hadn't been half-drunk and living in his truck at the time, he might have punched her in her skinny little face, told her to mind her man, and walked out.

But the truck wasn't running and he was out of choices. That was always the way, wasn't it? When a woman saw you down, she just pushed harder. Patty did, for sure, and old Rick had the dull, haunted eyes and the balding head to show for it. She insisted he watch the kids when they weren't in school. She insisted he vacuum three times a week, and it was his job to take the Glads out to the trash barrel and burn them.

Rick was a trash man, too. Abel wondered if he hadn't done his buddy a favor this morning, putting him out of his misery.

This river house was a good place to do it, too. The double-wide sat nuzzled in along the river on fifty acres that Patty's dad had given her when he died, in a clearing that wasn't no bigger than a high school football field. It was connected to the rest of the world by a trail of a road cutting through a thousand acres of forest all around. The only neighbors in a few miles were the new folks at the top of the mountain. Ethan somebody...Galloway, that was it...and his wife. Their place was the only other house on this road and it was a lot nicer than this one – flat firm ground, plenty of sunshine up top. A nice chunk of land that wasn't down in a hole of a valley like this place.

Abel met Ethan Galloway once, when he was out walking on the road, and he wasn't impressed. They moved in from the city to play farmers, it seemed. His wife was a pretty thing. She reminded Abel of his own wife, back when she was alive. Long legs, strong-looking. Not one of those frail girls like Abel saw on TV, but slim and healthy. Quite the filly. He had remarked as much to Ethan, but the man's eyes had gone cold and he'd taken a step between the road and the house, just to make a point.

Like Abel was going to sprint over there and take the woman for himself.

Not a bad idea, but not worth fighting a man who looked and acted like he was in the prime of his life, either. Which Ethan did. He'd said he was in his forties, but it wouldn't take much to imagine him younger by a decade. He told Abel they had retired early and moved out here to enjoy life.

Abel had laughed at that. "Me, too," he'd said. "Retired early from the auction house."

Ethan had just accepted it, nodding that neat-clipped haircut and collared shirt. Dumbass.

If it wasn't for Ethan, Abel might have taken a swipe at sweet little...what did Ethan say her name was? Winny or something? No...Quinn, that was it. Sounded exotic. He thought she'd be a fine one, once he made her understand that he wasn't no trash man. Not like Rick. Not like his Pap.

Still, it didn't hurt to look at her now and then, did it? Abel felt the stirrings and suddenly that was a good idea. It would pass the time until Patty came home and he found out how she was going to react to her missing husband. He turned away from the river and the house and his buddy Rick, left the coyotes behind, and headed for the steep road that would take him up the mountain.

Halfway across the mud pit that passed for a front yard, he stopped. Turned back toward the house and squinted, thinking. His mind was nagging at him, telling him to remember something. What was it?

The blood? He'd killed Rick in the kitchen, but he hadn't cleaned up yet. Time enough for that later. No, this was something else. Some little thing itching at the edge of his thoughts. It wasn't about Rick. He didn't think it was about the folks up the mountain, either.

A picture flashed lightly through the fog of his thoughts. It was Patty, in her bedroom, telling him to get out or she would call Rick to *escort him off the premises*. Abel had laughed at her, and she had gone to the closet.

Thinking about it, he grinned.

She had pulled one of those little safe boxes down from the closet. It was gray and black, with buttons. She had stared him dead in the eye and said, "Don't make me shoot you, old man."

That little incident told him two things – that Patty was not a woman to be trusted, and that she had a gun. The first one he already knew. The second...well, he didn't think it would be too hard to get into that box if he wanted.

He was pretty sure he wanted. In fact, he was kind of mad that he hadn't remembered it before now. He turned back toward the house, after one long glance up the mountain.

No hurry. He had time. With the storm rolling in, he didn't think Ethan and Quinn would be going anywhere. Maybe two husbands needed to die today. He could see himself comforting poor little Quinn when her husband didn't come home.

Chapter Two

Quinn Galloway opened her eyes and stared at the ceiling where it was banded with dim early morning daylight. Something felt wrong. She glanced toward the windows. The early morning light glowed brightly around the thick closed drapes, highlighting a strip down the center. The strip was blue and cold.

She lay very still and tried to figure out why her skin was goose-pimpled and icy, in spite of the warm quilts piled high on top of her, and why tension curled in her belly like a snake. Her heart was banging hard against her ribs. She rubbed her chest. It hurt like she'd been holding her breath. The sheets were cool around her ankles.

She could smell the odd mixture of fabric softener and oil from last night. Ethan had been cleaning his guns and placing them neatly into the locked cabinet in the corner. She glanced at it now, a hulking, shadow-shrouded thing in the far corner. She had objected at first, telling him that gun cabinets didn't belong in her bedroom, but that was a rule she'd invented on the fly. The truth was, she didn't like the idea of weapons so close to her head, filling up so much of her safe space. The bedroom wasn't for cold steel and gunpowder – it was for soft linens and shelter.

And to be honest, she didn't like the way he caressed the metal when he performed this chore. She didn't like the look on his face, the way he got so absorbed in the weapons that he sometimes didn't even hear when she spoke to him. It was to be expected – he liked guns, but he hadn't owned any back in Atlanta. Now that they were here, he had his excuse.

Ethan, in his patient way, had suggested that the gun cabinet would look worse taking up a whole corner of the living room, and she had relented, knowing he was right. She still objected, but somewhere along the way she had stopped arguing about it. Choose your battles, her mother always told her, and she did. This was nothing but a minor skirmish in the grand scheme of things, not worth missiles or minefields.

She lay very still and listened closely for any hint of what was off-kilter, but only heard the faint *tick* of ice on the walls of the cabin and the ominous creaks and groans of occasional wind gusts. The room was cold - the fire must be low in the living room.

Eventually, after a few minutes of staring at the ceiling and listening, it dawned on her. The house was empty. She hated to do it, but she threw back her covers and sat on the edge of the bed. A shiver ran down her spine, and not just because the chill billowed around her bare knees. Ethan was gone.

She could feel it in the weightless silence of the house, and her senses told her she was right - no smell of thick smoked bacon in the frying pan, no radio tuned to *KAFE, The Morning Drink of Good Music!* No movement, no soft whistling while he stood in the middle of the kitchen floor, waving his favorite red spatula and debating whether to make pancakes or eggs. No, he was gone.

A snowstorm was rolling in, too, she remembered. The well-dressed and gleeful newscaster had chattered about it for nearly twenty minutes last night. What had she called it? Winter Storm Leo? It was expected to drop nearly two feet of snow on the area by midnight tonight, and another foot tomorrow.

Quinn wasn't looking forward to it. As isolated as they were, nearly fifteen miles from small-town Randolph, VA, they knew to be prepared - and they were - but she still didn't like being cut off from the rest of the world. The thought of it made her nervous.

She slipped off the bed, into her slippers and robe. On her way past the bureau she snagged a tortoise shell clip and collected her hair into a quick, loose bun. When she opened the bedroom door, the light spilling in from the bright kitchen at the other end of the hall made her wince.

For half a second she paused, just looking. She didn't want to go into the main part of the house, even entertained the thought of going back to bed. Ethan wasn't home, but surely he'd come walking in before long. He might even be cold enough to join her under the quilts. They could snuggle.

She knew better, of course. Her husband loved his morning walks and he always, always came home full of energy. He was an early bird, and he proved it every day. His dark hair would be messed up from his toboggan and his cheeks would still be red from the cold. He would be full of stories about the beavers down near the river, or how fast the new calves were growing in the field that butted up to their farm. He might even have pictures, and she might even look at them, but only after a hot cup of coffee.

The warmer air drew her to the front of the house. As she walked through the kitchen, she glanced out the wide double windows to the world outside. Snowflakes were already falling, lazy soft things that nevertheless foreshadowed the storm to come. Icy grass spiked the yard and the fields beyond. At the edge of the woods, beyond the low-slung barn, she could see a few does grazing. Something blue swooped past the window, inches from her nose and vanished before she could see it. A jay, probably. They and the cardinals were forever fighting over the seed Ethan put out for them.

All in all, it was a peaceful scene. So why wasn't her tension melting away? Ethan most likely just lost track of time. He did that sometimes. He'd get caught up in watching the wildlife and forget to come in until he was stiff with cold. He'd be here eventually, dusting his hands together - or trying to stick them under her robe to make her screech - and then he would tell her about the owl or the otters or whatever creatures he'd seen. She would smack his hands away, pour him a cup of coffee (*KAFE!*) and then he would make breakfast.

Logically she knew all of this, but reminding herself didn't quiet the ping of alarm in the back of her mind. She checked the time. It was after eight.

There was nothing to be alarmed about, not at all. This happened all the time now. She had only recently gotten used to these slow, easy mornings, after the hustle of working in the city. No more scrambling out the door, no more traffic, no more trolling for parking while she kept one eye on the dashboard clock. No, these days were good. And now that she and Ethan were officially retired, they would be good for a long time to come.

She walked to the counter and shook out two of the anxiety pills that sat in a bottle there. This was something else their country adventure was helping – she wasn't taking nearly as many of these as she had in the city.

Quinn had been nervous about Ethan's dream farm in the beginning, although she really had no reason to object. If he had always wanted to live in the country, who was she to argue? Neither of them had family to leave behind - hers was small in the first place, and her parents had died, one after another, while she was in college. His was nonexistent. He had decided that he wanted this place about a decade into their marriage and didn't mention it for another two years after that. She didn't know what sparked the idea, beyond his insistence that he had always wanted a place in the country, even when he was a child. In any case, she had balked at first, sure that neither of them would enjoy leaving behind the comforts and convenience of the city.

But he had worn her down, little by little. He'd made it all seem so romantic - fresh eggs from fat, happy hens, a soft-eyed cow, maybe even horses to ride in the summer. He promised a river full of fresh trout, which she had tasted once and loved. He promised long walks down meandering trails and funny side trips into a nearby picturesque, American small town. In his eyes, it was the perfect dream, and like a drip of water drilling through stone, he had made his dream hers.

She had teased him, saying that Norman Rockwell was his spirit animal, and he had laughed and nodded in agreement. But the sparkle of it all was alive in his eyes, and eventually she'd felt it, too, in spite of her fears.

Not that he disregarded her, not at all. Her anxiety was an established fact in their marriage, something he helped her work around on a day to day basis. He reminded her to take her meds, and he rushed home when the shadows threatened to solidify and choke her. He held her in the night when the world went quiet and her thoughts told her that none of her happiness would last, that the next time she stepped out of the house something unthinkable would happen. He was there every time she felt hostile eyes on her, giving her hard, quick hugs and telling her that they were imaginary ghosts of impossible events. He was right, every time.

In the end, one of the big reasons that she relented was his promise of open spaces and fewer people. That, in fact, was her dream. He told her that he could make it happen, and he had. In the space of a single year they had found the farm, traveled to inspect it, sold their home in Atlanta and made their way north to a brand new kind of adventure.

She and Ethan had closed the deal on the little cabin just last summer and they only moved in during November, just in time for the tiniest thanksgiving celebration ever. It was just the two of them, surrounded by boxes and bags, sitting cross-legged on the floor in front of the fireplace. They had pancakes, because her big roasting pans were packed away. In her opinion, it was the best thanksgiving of their lives together.

She walked back into the bedroom and dressed. Jeans and a t-shirt, another easy thing. No more heels and skirts and pantyhose, and for that she was eternally grateful. A thick sweater over the t-shirt, just until she warmed up. She wasn't old - only forty two - but on mornings like this, the cold made her feel closer to seventy. No matter - she would shake it off. In fact, she decided, pulling her hair into a more proper ponytail, she would make Ethan breakfast for a change.

Bacon first, because Ethan liked his eggs fried in the grease, and then a quick mixing of drop biscuits and she slid them into the oven. She fried her eggs when the bacon was done, but since she didn't know when he'd be home, she waited to put his into the skillet. Biscuits, eggs, bacon. Breakfast was fabulous, if she did say so herself.

Yet. He still wasn't home. She ate quickly, cleaned up after herself and covered the skillet. Pushed it to the back burner, still warm. Looked out the window to see the jays still fighting, the deer long gone. Day was brightening over the blue Appalachians, thawing the frosty grass a little. Not much, though. The sky was heavy with storm clouds. Leo would be here soon.

The phone rang, startling her. For a moment she simply stared at it, not quite comprehending the sound. The kitchen was suddenly too bright and the floor was cold under her bare feet. She tiptoed her way to the phone on the wall - no cell phones out here in the mountains - and put out her hand to answer it. For a second she faltered, her belly seizing as if the phone receiver were a hot skillet. A dreadful fear rose up, threatening to choke her.

Don't answer it.

Then, with a shake of her head and a quick, deep breath, she swallowed down her sudden nerves and jerked the receiver off its cradle. Looked at it, wondering what in the world was wrong with her this morning.

"Hello? Ethan?" The voice was tiny and shrill in the cold light of the kitchen. She put the phone to her ear.

Don't answer it. "Hello?"

A moment of silence. Then, "Quinn?"

"Yes." Her voice was brittle. Her throat ragged. She swallowed hard and tried again. "This is she."

"Quinn, it's Marvin."

"Hello."

Her mind snapped to, all at once. She shook her head again. Why was Ethan's doctor calling here during office hours? That wasn't right. Doctors didn't call people at home, did they? "Ethan isn't here right now," she said.

"We spoke yesterday, and I have some more information about his diagnosis. I was wondering if he could come back to the city and stop by my office tomorrow."

"Diagnosis?" The dread twisted into a solid beast in her gut. Sour. Savage. Clawing its way into her mind. "What diagnosis?"

"The Alzheimer's? He told you, didn't he?" Marvin's voice was suddenly hesitant.

She stared at a spot out the window, where the neatly cleared front walkway met the sharp white edge of snow, and tried to make sense of the question. Marvin Scopes was not only Ethan's doctor, but a family friend. He and his wife Annette had come to their house for supper several times in Atlanta, and Quinn knew their two daughters from school. The girls, red-haired twin beauties, had been smart kids, easy to teach. Marvin and Annette were good people, offering their time and attention to several charities in the city.

Ethan, who didn't like doctors in the first place, had made an exception for Marvin, and even though they now lived five hundred miles to the north, he insisted that he would rather fly down to Marvin's office in Atlanta for his yearly checkup than brave the small clinic in the nearby town of Randolph, Virginia. He'd done this very thing last Friday, taking a quick round-trip flight south for the day.

"His checkup?" she asked. Her mouth didn't seem capable of forming the words.

"Yes. We found some anomalies that indicate early onset Alzheimer's." Marvin's voice softened a little. "Oh, dear. He did tell you, didn't he?"

Quinn shook her head. He hadn't. "No."

The dread became something else, something dark and hot behind her belly button. She placed a hand there, pressed inward. Her gaze slid to the small kitchen table, where her latest project waited patiently for her. "No, Marvin. He didn't."

Marvin made a small noise on the other end of the phone, far away in Atlanta. "Have him call me, will you?"

"I will."

"Have a good day, Quinn," Marvin said. His voice was still soft, but now it was full of something that sounded a lot like sadness, or maybe worry.

"Thank you." She hung up the phone, placing the receiver on its hanging base in slow motion. Her eyes were still on the table, and she followed her own gaze there, shuffling slowly to the chair she'd pulled out just a few minutes ago, and sank into it. She grabbed the tail of her sweater, balled her hands into cloth-filled fists in her lap. Stared at them.

Alzheimer's.

Chapter Three

E than hadn't said a word. He never mentioned it. During supper the night before, she noticed that the lines around his eyes had gone deeper, but she had chalked that up to his not sleeping well. For the last week, he had tossed and turned a lot. She wondered at the time if the line of winter storms rolling through was messing with his sinuses, causing headaches. Or maybe, she remembered guessing, he was worried about something that he would discuss with her when he was ready.

Now she knew. It had never occurred to her that his restlessness and his checkup were related. He was the healthiest person she knew.

He hadn't told her.

She stared out the window at the jays again. Her throat felt tight and hot.

He hadn't told her.

Every time the thought touched her mind, it felt like a punch to the gut. Underneath the vicious fear that clawed at her chest, she felt something even worse - betrayal. It wasn't the beast of dread like before, but something smaller and more slippery. Something as cold as the floor under her feet. It skipped upward along her ribs and needled at the edge of her heart. Nausea threatened her vision for a moment, before she took a deep shaky breath and blinked it away.

She reached for the boxes of photos on the far corner of the table, and flipped through some of them. Her project. Ethan's hobby. The photos were from all over the world, every trip they'd taken in their twenty years together. A history of their life. A history of their history.

Every summer, they had taken two journeys from their little tract house in the Atlanta suburbs to somewhere that felt exotic to them for one reason or another. Trips to Brazil, Yosemite, Las Vegas, Madrid. Every jaunt to a new world had strengthened their marriage and given them fresh excitement for the rest of the year. Ethan had catalogued almost every one of their moments in those places, constantly snapping bits and pieces of a foreign world. He wanted to remember. Needed to remember.

His life before Quinn had been chaotic and jagged, with too many forfeits to count. His parents were gone before he knew them, dead in an airplane crash just outside of New York City. After that, his life became a series of losses as he wended his way through the foster care system. People left behind, memories eclipsed.

So he had determined to remember everything of their lives. "You are my second chance," he'd said at their wedding, his suit too hot and his hands shaking in front of fifty people. That crooked, charming smile on his face.

And then he had set out to do just that – remember everything. From crazy, colorful bazaar stalls in Italy to a zoo in London. All of it was right here, piled in mounds on their dining room table in Virginia. How many trips had there been? Forty? Fifty? Ethan could name and date every single one, but he wasn't patient enough to put his thousands of pictures into their proper albums and boxes. Now that they were settled, Quinn had wanted to get the photos into some sort of order.

She shifted in her chair. It squeaked, like a wounded bird. Her gaze went to the window again, to the back yard. A lone jay dive-bombed the empty bird feeder, scaring away some small, fat brown bird on the banister. She wondered where Ethan was, and when he might come home. Then she wondered if she should ask him about the call, or let him tell her in his own time. A diagnosis of Alzheimer's of all things, would strike him down faster than almost anything else. His memories were everything to him. Losing them would be his own personal version of hell.

She sat there, watching lazy snowflakes swirl. Minutes ticked by in silence. She realized after a while that she was waiting, listening for Ethan to come stomping through the door. She had no interest in moving from her place. She needed answers. Information. Reassurance. She needed these things from Ethan, and he wasn't here.

Eventually she roused herself to get a cup of coffee. There was nearly a full pot - Ethan had made it that morning and left it for her after his single cup. It was bitter and strong now, and she savored it. After that, she was able to bring in an armful of firewood from the crate on the porch and build up the fire, which had dwindled to a few orange embers in the fireplace. Then she stood beside it, her forehead against the tall wooden mantle, with her hands in her pockets. Still listening. Her throat hurt. She was tired.

Marvin had mentioned more information. Maybe it turned out to be nothing. Maybe it was a mistake, and he was calling to tell Ethan about the stupid technician who didn't know how to read the test results. That was probably it.

That had to be it, and she made herself believe it to keep her panic at bay. She would ask him about it when he came home, and he would explain.

He hadn't told her because he wasn't sure, of course. Marvin would have said something like, "Don't worry, Ethan. We'll run these tests again." Ethan would have waited, so that she wouldn't worry for nothing.

So why wasn't he here now? Why wasn't he here, waiting for that phone call? Where was he?

The rooster crowed from the pen in the back, startling her. It was enough to reset her spiraling thoughts and bring her back to this moment. There wasn't a thing she could do until her husband got home and told her what was going on, now was there? She would have to wait, and that was OK. She chuckled at herself, pushed her worry down deep, and went to feed them.

This was one of the ways she dealt with her anxiety – by putting things into mental boxes, keeping them out of the way until it was time to deal with them. If she didn't do that, she would be a sniveling mess all the time.

Halfway across to the rickety little lean-to shed, the panic came back. It slammed her like a blow to the head. Her feet stumped to a halt. She turned, slowly, trying to figure out what. What was wrong? What new thing had happened? She fought to think, fought the urge to run back to the house, and momentarily ignored the chickens that had come rushing out to greet her, pecking at the fence and squawking for their breakfast.

The feeling of something wrong clawed at her again. Why? Was it that she was outside now? That happened sometimes, when the sheer vastness of the outside world threatened to overwhelm her. It had been that way even back home, in Atlanta. Some days it took all the fight in her to keep walking. But this felt different...more like she was missing some vital piece of information.

The dogs. She stood in the center of the back yard, between the deck and the barn, and turned her head toward the kennel and fenced run that banked the left side of the cabin. Retro and Burns, Ethan's large and playful German Shepherds, were standing at the fence, watching her. They were still pups, really. Big and goofy, not quite a year old. When Burns saw her looking, he chuffed. He wanted breakfast, too.

Why hadn't Ethan taken them with him? He always took them. Always.

She squeezed her cold fingers into fists, willing herself to stand still. Burns chuffed again, raising one giant paw to the chain link fence and watching her steadily. Retro, on the other hand, was hopping back and forth, wanting to play, snuffing Burns's ear with his nose and yipping. Every once in a while he would go still and glance toward the woods, but then get distracted by his brother again.

Think, Quinn. It's fine. It's just the dogs. Ethan forgot them. That's all.

She looked at them, and that helped her thumping heart. They were beautiful dogs, caramel colored with the classic black saddle and large, black-tipped ears. Ethan had gone to pick out a pup - one pup - from a private breeder last September. He had come back with three. She remembered staring, open-mouthed as he opened the rear door of their SUV and puppies had come spilling out. Then she had laughed, because she'd won that bet. She knew he wouldn't stop at one.

But three? He had batted his dark blue eyes at her and explained that the pups were kept in an old sewer drain in the breeder's muddy back yard. How it had been raining, and he couldn't just leave them there, could he? No, of course he couldn't.

And the poor babies' coats had backed him up - they were matted and stinking with something Quinn didn't want to think about, much less touch. One of the pups - the smallest and weakest of the three - had a large gash along his hindquarter. It looked infected.

"This one is mine, then," she'd told him. "This little guy right here."

"Girl."

"Fine. Girl, then. She's mine." Quinn had scooped up the injured pup, shot him a smile as the warm little nose nuzzled against her neck, and then carried her inside for a good hot bath.

The pup was too scrawny, too weak. Quinn named her Daisy, fed her via dropper for three days, then took her to the vet. An hour later, with real sadness in his eyes, he was putting her down. Then he had asked for the contact information of the breeder, promising Quinn that it would never happen again.

So only Retro and Burns were left, and they had grown enough to make up for the weight of their little sister. They ate enough to make up for her, too.

But not this morning. She walked over to check their bowls, and was completely shocked to see that they were empty. They watched her and whined. They needed food, and they needed to be set free. They needed to run. Why hadn't Ethan taken them? He always took them. A small part of Quinn wanted to cry, but she swallowed it back, fed the chickens.

She was probably blowing things all out of proportion. She did that sometimes. Ethan might have gone to help their elderly neighbor Cap with some farm chore or another. Or maybe he had gone to town. She walked to the side of the house and checked the driveway. Nope, the truck was still there beside her SUV, frosted over and gathering fat flakes of new snow on the windshield. It hadn't been moved at all.

She walked back to the dog pen while she checked her coat pocket for her keys. Then she clicked the little fob and watched the waist high pen door swing open. The dogs exploded through the gate, falling all over each other and their own feet, racing to greet her. "Hey boys," she said softly. Retro started to jump, but she held out her hand, palm front, and he remembered. "Sit."

Both dog plopped onto the grass, their tails thumping. She smiled - Ethan was doing a good job, training them. They were smart pups, too, and they seemed to have a great connection with him. She reached down to scratch their ears, first Retro and then Burns, who tried to snap his head up and catch her hand. She felt his teeth graze her fingers and jerked back, out of his reach. He did that nearly every time, like he was trying to keep her there, petting him. It was one of the few things Ethan couldn't seem to train out of him. The best they could do, when he did it, was to stop petting.

Ethan had put their wide orange collars on them at some point, she noticed. It was hunting season, and he didn't want them to get shot accidentally. It didn't happen often around here, people were usually careful with their weapons, but it did happen. Cap had mentioned it, back in December when they'd first moved in, else they wouldn't have known either.

She was finding that there was a lot of nuance to the country life, and it was going to take some adjustment. From the jostle and buzz of Atlanta to the slow lull of a life in northern Virginia, well, it was a leap. But it was Ethan's dream.

She threw feed to the chickens and watched them scratch after it and cluck their appreciation. Then she turned and scanned the edge of the woods again.

The dogs were still sitting, so she snapped her fingers and said, "Go," releasing them to play. They took off across the field, chasing one another.

Their cabin sat on top of the mountain, a hundred yards from the cliffhugger road they took to get there. "Like a wedding cake centerpiece," Ethan had said, when they first saw it. Surrounded by fields on all sides, and then woods beyond that, the property seemed to float near the clouds. The woods went on a little and then fell away, down the mountainsides to the river. The only trees between the house and woods were a stand of cedars over to the west, near the gate.

Someone had chosen right – the site was a beautiful spot for a home. They could hear any car coming long before it got close, which had come in handy a couple of times when the less than friendly neighbors down in the hollow by the river had stumbled onto their property.

Quinn had long believed that everything had a Catch - if something good happened in her life, the Catch was bad. It worked the other way around, too – when something bad happened, she was usually able to see a silver lining of some sort, no matter how thin the lining or how dull the silver. But the Catch, when she thought of it capitalized like that, was usually bad.

Here in the land of open fields and peace and quiet, those neighbors were the Catch. It wasn't that they caused a lot of trouble, but Quinn was always aware that they were down there, and she was aware that they were the kind of neighbors that wouldn't last ten minutes in the tight-buttoned suburbs of Atlanta. They were a young family (she thought) with three kids, but there always seemed to be others staying in their house, too. She didn't know the dynamics, but she had wondered a few times where everybody slept.

They weren't a huge problem, but they liked to crank the music and get their drink on, as Ethan said, more days of the week than not. Mostly, they kept to themselves, and that was good. The kids were nice enough. Two boys and a girl, all between the ages of ten and fifteen, if she had to guess. They were the best of the family, and all three of them were well-mannered and cute. She watched them walk by every morning to get on the school bus at the bottom of the mountain. Their clothes were old, but clean, and they always waved when they spotted her at the window.

The parents were, she supposed, typical country folks. Sometimes Quinn and Ethan heard four wheelers and trucks gunning their engines and spinning out in the mud at all hours of the night. That was OK, it wasn't like they were in the front yard, but it was interesting. Wild and crazy was apparently the motto on those nights. Ethan had offered to go down, ask them to be quiet, but Quinn hadn't liked that idea at all. She couldn't say why, but she worried that the neighbors who kept to themselves might turn nasty if somebody tried to interrupt their good time.

The wind bit at her face. She lifted a hand to feel her frozen cheek and noticed that the dogs weren't close by anymore. She turned in a slow circle, scanning the dead yellow fields. The cedars stood tall and stark against a white sky chased by gray. The clouds were moving faster, carrying the storm. There was no sign of Ethan.

The dogs were bounding along the edge of the far field, wrestling and tripping over themselves as they ran. It was good for them to stretch their legs, good that they had so much space to run. Ethan loved big dogs, but he refused to have one back in Atlanta. He said it was cruel to keep them penned up in their little back yard, and she agreed. They didn't start looking for pets until they were sure about the move.

Retro saw her watching and came running across the field at breakneck speed. He slid to a stop near her feet, his tongue lolling and his breath whitening the cold air. "You ready for some breakfast?" she asked him. He stood up, sat again, and whined. His thick red tail brushed the grass until Burns wandered over and stepped on it. Retro jumped up, highly offended. Quinn laughed.

"Where is Ethan, boys?" she asked them, starting toward the house. The big blue trash can where he kept their food sat on the covered end of the back deck. Its orange ACE Hardware logo stood out in the shadows. She decided on her way across the yard to leave the two of them loose until he came home. She doubted they would be much use if there was real trouble, but having them around made her feel better.

The thought made her pause. Why would she be thinking about trouble? It was a perfectly quiet morning in rural Virginia. Everything was fine. "Get a grip, Quinn," she fussed. To shake off her growing dread, she turned and stomped back into the house, leaving the dogs to amuse themselves with squirrels and deer and whatever else dogs usually found fascinating. They wouldn't go anywhere - Ethan had trained them well.

Besides, she liked the idea of strangers meeting those teeth before they got to the house.

Inside she stripped off her outer clothes and made the bed and straightened the house, not that it needed it, and then she turned her attention to a project that she'd been putting off since before the move: their picture albums.

She didn't know why she wanted to do this right now. Maybe because she missed Ethan. Maybe, probably, the word Alzheimer's had something to do with it.

Even at home, during their average day-to-day, Ethan was a photo hound, snapping pics of anything and everything that caught his eye. Sometimes the subject was Quinn, sometimes it was a random stranger he noticed at the grocery store. He liked taking pictures of open markets, too. All those long stalls of food and fabric and people, there was no way he could resist. He was like one of those annoying artist types when he did that, taking nine pictures of the same thing because the light was different over there, or asking people to ignore him so that he could catch the 'local color', as he called it. Surprisingly, most of them obliged.

She laughed at him when he acted this way, calling him the *art-teest* and trying to make him wear an old beret she had picked up at a flea market somewhere. He'd slap it away and say it was silly, then go on to take the boxes and boxes of photos that she was staring at here on the dining room table. She had quite a job ahead of her.

The boxes were half-stacked, half-tossed on the corner of the wooden farmhouse table nearest the wall. She dug them out of the closet the night before, promising to get them sorted by the end of the week. It was only Tuesday, but she still didn't think she would make the deadline.

Ethan didn't know why she bothered, and to be honest she wasn't sure, either, but it was a good way to get her mind off...well, things. She would swim around in their memories for a while, then Ethan would come home and explain, and then she would make a roast for supper. She would make him promise to never do that again without leaving a note. He would agree, and they would snuggle in for their long winter's night.

She saw one of the dogs race past the kitchen window and remembered that they were loose. Hurrying to the back door, she opened it just in time to see both of them headed right for the gate. "Retro!" she called. "Burns!"

They skidded to a halt.

"Come," she said. They did.

The gate gave way to a field and several outbuildings, but that wasn't the problem. The fields were theirs, but beyond that, if the dogs kept going, another farmer's field butted up to theirs. Those fields were full of new calves. The last thing Quinn needed today was a phone call from a farmer telling her that her dogs were gnawing on his livelihood. She called them to her and locked them up in their kennel. They flopped down in the hay and looked ashamed.

Chapter Four

By the time the afternoon sky began to darken, she had given up trying to concentrate on her task and gone to sit in his big recliner near the window. This window offered the best view of the property in general, with emphasis on the gravel road that ran past the house. There was no traffic, and the kids had long since made their meandering way toward home, not bothering to wave at her after their long day at school.

A half peanut butter sandwich sat uneaten on a saucer beside the chair, and her coffee cup was empty again. Good, because she was drinking way too much of that today. There was still no sign of Ethan, and she was thinking about calling their friend Cap. Maybe Ethan was there, helping with some chore or another. Quinn didn't think that was the case, because he would have called by now. But it was the first thing she thought of, without thinking the unthinkable.

And the unthinkable was gaining ground. Accident? Animal attack? Either of those things were very possible. Quinn was well aware that in the country, things like this happened. Ethan could be lying somewhere with a broken leg or a damaged head, if he fell on one of the paths on the west side of the property and rolled into the ravine that cut sharply through the earth and led, eventually, to the river.

She stared out the window toward the road, wishing for Ethan to come in, strolling across the fields, patting the cedars as he went by. He loved those trees. "Old men standing guard," he called them. "Been here since before the Revolutionary." Of course, neither of them knew that for sure, but he liked to imagine it that way.

Once, not too long before their wedding, he he'd bought a bottle of wine and led her out to the deck at their house in Atlanta. It had been early afternoon, she remembered. They had just finished lunch. There in the lawn chairs, between sips, he had gone over everything, his whole life. Every single foster family, every single friend he'd ever had, every time they had stood together against the world.

When his voice finally trailed off, her eyes were bleary and the sun was starting to come up. She was flattered - and exhausted - by the end of his story. Flattered because he had chosen to share all of it with her. She could tell that the time was a way to grieve. A way to purge any unhappy memories, dismiss any missteps, and cement his life before Quinn in a kind of memorial block. He would, she knew, put that block away now and let it be. And that's what he had done.

Maybe he was out in the woods now, remembering, the way he had then. He wasn't sharing this time, but maybe the idea of losing his memories was too painful for him. Maybe he needed time. But it would be dark soon. When was he coming home?

She couldn't just sit here anymore. She put down her sandwich and grabbed up the phone, quickly dialing Cap's number before she could rethink it. She knew it was a long shot, but it was the easiest place to start. He answered on the third ring, croaking a loud, "What?"

"Cap? Is Ethan there?" she asked. "This is Quinn."

"I know who it is," he yelled back at her. She couldn't help a smile. He was the kind of old man who never really trusted the crazy technology of these new-fangled telephones. If he yelled, it worked better. "He ain't here."

"Oh, OK. Sorry to bother you." She fought the urge to cry, even though she'd already known the answer – the distance to Cap's, on the other side of the mountain, was too far to walk. Ethan would have taken the truck.

"Heard some gunshots up your way this morning," Cap said. "Figured it was either Ethan or those mossyheads down in the holler," he said.

She frowned. Ethan wouldn't have gone hunting, she didn't think. "When this morning? What time?"

"Bout five, I guess. You know I don't sleep no more."

"Sure, I understand." Her heart was drumming again. She eyed her pills, across the open room on the kitchen counter. She sank back down onto Ethan's chair and gripped one arm with her free hand. "Cap, thanks for the information. I've got to go."

"Sure, sure. Tell Ethan to come around, either tomorrow morning or the next. Got a gutter down at the back of the house, and ladders ain't my friend these days."

"Of course. I'll tell him." If I can find him, she thought.

They hung up, and she immediately went to the closet and put her coat back on. She stepped into her heavy rubber boots, and slipped on her gloves. Only then did she open the front door, grab the flashlight off the bookshelf by the door, and step out onto the wide front porch.

She stopped at the top step and looked around. Looked at the road, followed it with her eyes. It went to the house at the bottom, she knew, and stopped at the river. She should go there, and ask those people if they had seen Ethan.

She knew she wouldn't. Part of it was general anxiety, but another part, the part that looked at the shadowy, rough road that disappeared down into the dark trees, told her that going there would be a bad idea. A very, very bad idea.

It had started to snow again, those thick gray clouds from earlier finally dumping more than two inches of snow since she'd put the dogs away. It was colder, too, and she was glad for the fur lining of her rubber boots. Still on the porch, she reached into her pocket and pressed the button on the key fob. Twenty seconds later, the dogs came racing around the side of the house and thumping up the wood stairs, falling over each other to get to her. They almost knocked her down before they got stopped completely.

"Retro!" she snapped. "Burns!"

They sat immediately, snowflakes clinging to their dark fur. Burns whined a little.

She felt bad that she'd forgotten to pen them up this morning. What if something had happened to them? They could have been hit by a car, or lost in the woods. Did dogs get lost? Couldn't they just follow their own trail back home? She didn't know, and now wasn't the time to worry about it.

She released them to go play for a few minutes, letting them get their energy out by chasing each other around the front yard for a while. They tackled each other and snapped at the snow, making her smile. Finally, she called them back to her. She was running out of time.

"Retro, stay." She said it firmly, then curled her fingers around Burns's collar and led him around the side of the house to the pen. She put him inside, made sure the gate was locked, and went back to where Retro waited. "Come on, boy," she said. "You're with me."

This wasn't the Catch. It couldn't be. The snow was beautiful, the night was crisp, and the air was fresh and clean-smelling. Her own growing fear aside, there was nothing to worry about, and when she found Ethan she would see just how foolish she had been.

She spent a moment or two looking around, then started off, deciding to follow Ethan's daily footsteps. Every morning he crossed the road and walked across the field, his tall form stark against the frosty trees. If she was awake, she watched him until he disappeared into the woods on the far side of the property. After that...well, she didn't know exactly where he went, so she would be winging it.

She clicked on the flashlight. "Come, Retro," she said, her words loud in the silence. The commands still felt foreign to her, a girl who had grown up playing with the mutts in her family, instead of teaching them anything. Of course, those dogs were nowhere near as smart or expensive as these two, and her family had never depended on them for security, either. She was glad about that - the goofballs her mom tended to bring home probably weren't capable of protecting anyone from anything. Retro and Burns, on the other hand, were their first-warning system and last-resort weapons, if the situation got out of control. That was the point of the key fob release, after all.

Her feet crunched across the grass, then rattled the gravel in the road as she made her way toward the woods. Another thirty minutes and it would be dark. She was glad she remembered the light.

It was still snowing, too. The flakes lit on her nose and in her eyelashes. By the time she got to the edge of the woods and paused, looking in between the trees, her hair was wet. The end of her ponytail swung in and caught under the collar of her coat. She shivered. "Well, boy, let's go."

The trees over her head cut off the last of the daylight, leaving her in total darkness. Retro pressed against her leg. She loved both dogs, but had bonded more with Retro these last few months for some reason that she couldn't actually name. Maybe it was his playful nature - he was less on guard than Burns, even when he was supposed to be training. A clown, Ethan called him, and Quinn had to agree. Retro's eyes glowed with a sparkle that made Quinn think he was laughing. Still, he learned his lessons well enough and he was a sweet dog.

Now, close to her right hand, he paused in their walk and chuffed lightly toward the woods. She redirected the light - his fur was climbing to a thick ruff along his spine.

She stopped breathing, and wouldn't start again until he relaxed his stance. She knew not to speak - he would take her voice as permission to relax and wait for further instructions, and she didn't want that. She wanted him on edge, if there was anything in these woods that could harm her.

She watched him closely. He took a couple of steps away from her, toward a particularly dark area of the trees. Through those trees, if her sense of direction was correct, was the road that led down to the river. She didn't see any headlights, though. She didn't hear a car engine. He raised his nose and sniffed at the cold air, then sneezed. She smiled at that, then pulled him back to her side. Somewhere off in the darkness a soft thump startled her. Snow, falling off a branch.

She hoped.

"Retro," she said, "We've got to find Ethan. Where is he, boy?"

Shining her light around her, she saw a trail of sorts leading through a less dense part of the trees. Her light hit twin reflections and a deer bounded away, into the cover of the foliage and brush. She waited for more, but this one appeared to be alone. "Let's go," she said to Retro.

She followed the trail, slowly, hoping that this was the way Ethan went every day, instead of just a random wildlife track to the river at the bottom of the mountain. The leaves still rustled under her feet, but not as loudly with the snow wetting them down. Retro pressed against her leg. As she walked, she flashed her light all around, scaring a bird here and there but getting a good view of the entire area. There was no sign of Ethan, or of him having come through here.

Behind her, in the direction of the house, she heard Burns bark. Once, twice. She thought she heard him whine. When she paused, Retro kept going, sniffing at the air.

Should she keep going, or go back to see what Burns was barking at? It could be that he was just mad - he'd been left behind, after all. If she kept going, would she find Ethan? He could be just beyond the next stand of trees, and if she turned back now she might miss finding him by mere feet.

But the slog through the woods felt like a waste of time, now that she was out here. Call it a hunch, call it her mental connection to her husband, but she didn't think she would find him in the woods.

She realized that she was already thinking of him as if he were gone for good. She didn't know why, and it was a stupid way to think. Her Ethan would never leave her without explanation, and he was strong and wise to the ways of the forest, even after years in the suburbs. She didn't think he would have gotten hurt badly, but it was possible. How could she know?

Her thoughts were starting to scramble. She shook her head and heaved a sigh.

Retro pulled the leash a little - Ethan had never quite broken him of that - but she held still. Then she scanned the woods once more, flashing the beam from tree trunk to tree trunk just to be sure, and started back toward the house.

She decided that she would check on Burns, then check the southern, western, and northern tree lines. She wouldn't go into the woods again, just shine the light from the edge of the field. Enough to reassure herself. Then, if Ethan was still missing, she would call nine-one-one. It was all she could think of to do.

Retro wasn't ready to stop exploring. He bounced and pulled until she got tired of fighting him and unclipped the lead. Surprisingly enough, he bounded off toward home. She sped up a little. She didn't like the feeling of being in these woods by herself. Stupid dog.

"Ethan, where are you?" she asked the night. An owl hooted somewhere off to her left.

When she broke free of the woods again, she glanced around the field, then checked the area around the house. The living room lights glowed warmly. She could see Burns, his feet on top of the fence, wanting out of his cage. Retro was standing in the center of the front yard, staring intently at something down the mountain, toward the mossyhead neighbors. She watched him duck his head a little, crouching. He was still a pup, but from here he looked vicious.

What did he see?

She took a step closer, then caught movement from the corner of her eye.

A man, standing in the middle of the road, barely discernible in the darkness around him.

Chapter Five

S he didn't recognize him immediately. He wore dark clothes. From here he looked like he might have a beard, too, but she couldn't be sure about that. The dim light glanced off his face, showing that he was watching Retro.

Then she saw him lift his arm, and her heart caught in her throat. Was he holding a gun? It looked like it - his stance, the way he lifted his chin, and the direction he was pointing - either he was casting a spell or aiming a weapon at her dog.

Anger battled with fear in her chest. Before one or the other could win she brought the flashlight up and blinded him with it. "Who's there?" she called.

His arm came up and blocked the beam, so she shifted the light to shine just above his head. She was right - he had a beard, a scraggy looking thing that reached almost to his chest. He wasn't skinny, exactly, but he wasn't a big man either. He didn't look healthy. Most importantly, when he brought his hand up she could see clearly that he was armed, with a small black handgun.

He shoved it into his pocket and turned her way. In front of the house, Retro relaxed his stance and trotted toward her.

The man didn't answer.

"Who are you?" she asked, still keeping her distance. It was obvious from the man's reaction that he hadn't seen her there. At least he put his gun away.

"Just walking, lady," the man said. His voice was reedy and kind of high.

"Why did you pull a gun on my dog, mister?"

The man took a step in her direction. "Stay there," she said. She wasn't armed at all, but he wouldn't know that. For all he could tell, she had a rifle by her side.

"I thought he was going to attack me."

She didn't believe a word of that. Retro was simply standing his ground on their property, making no move toward the guy. "Not unless I tell him to - should I?"

For half a second, she was impressed with how commanding she sounded.

The man shuffled his feet in the gravel, and she brought her flashlight into his eyes again. "What's your business out here?"

"I told you, I'm just going for a walk."

His whiny tone disgusted her a little, but she pushed that feeling aside. "Who are you?"

"Abel Welch. I'm staying with Patty and Rick."

He pointed down into the hollow, and she understood that Patty and Rick were the neighbors with three kids and too many house guests. This must be one of them.

She didn't say anything for a moment. She just watched him. He wasn't moving toward her, which was good. But he also wasn't moving back toward home, which was bad. The way he stood made her think of a cop, pulling someone over. Arms crossed, chest out, like he was the one who should be asking questions. Suddenly she had no doubt that if not for the threat of her nonexistent gun, he would be pushing his luck a lot more. She didn't know how she knew it, but it was as true as her name.

Folks around here prided themselves on being neighborly, but that only applied during daylight hours. If a person got caught sneaking around at night, they were going to be questioned, most likely at the point of a gun. Most people knew this, and Quinn didn't have any problem letting this man think she was carrying.

Her problem was that he was between her and the house.

Retro reached her and poked his cold nose into her hand. "Good boy," she murmured, scratching him behind the ear. The action calmed her a little, and reminded her that she wasn't alone. To the man she said, "You might want to head on home now."

He held up a hand. "Sure, sure. I'll be doing that."

He didn't move right away. She saw him glance toward the house. His eyes stopped somewhere near the vehicles - her SUV and Ethan's truck - parked near the road. Had he been planning to break into them? She had no idea. She was just glad that she was outside to see him before he could do any damage. "Go on, now. It's best if you don't come around here at night."

"Well..." He drew the word out, still not making a move to go away. "It seems that I'm on a state-maintained road. That's public property."

"Yessir. And if you had just been walking by, I wouldn't have said a word. But you didn't, did you? You stopped to take a look around. Why would you do that, Mr. Abel Welch?"

She was amazed that her voice sounded so steady, considering the fact that she was...what? Not scared, exactly. Nervous, yes. Angry? A little. But not scared. She wished Ethan was here to handle this, but he wasn't, and maybe she was a little mad at him, too.

But she thought she could handle this guy, as long as he didn't make any sudden moves.

He didn't answer, but he did turn her way. Then she saw him sway a little, and realized that he was drinking. Of course he was - that's all they seemed to do down at that ratty old double-wide. At least, that's all the adults seemed to do. Why would he be any different? She knew she was making ugly assumptions, and she didn't care. She just hoped he didn't call her bluff.

That's exactly what he was doing, though. He didn't turn around and go home, like she hoped. He simply stood there, blocking her way to safety and showing no plans to move. Her fingers tightened around the flashlight. It was a heavy red Mag Lite, nearly two feet long and made of metal. The kind that cops carried. She could use it to defend herself if she had to, but she was mostly relying on his assumption that she had a gun. "Go on home, now, Mr. Welch."

"I think I'll finish my walk," he said. His voice didn't sound so reedy now. It was deeper, more belligerent.

"Then move along. There is nothing for you to see here."

Did he chuckle? Was that a laugh she heard? "What if I don't?" he asked her. "It's not like you can call the cops from the middle of a field, now, can you?"

She shifted the flashlight to her other hand and reached into her pocket. Her keys were snuggled into the bottom corner. She found the button and pressed it without looking away. A moment later, she heard a soft squeak.

Abel Welch heard it too, and turned around again, just in time to see Burns explode from the gate, snarling. Retro took the hint and ran, too. They would meet, just about where the intruder was standing. Quinn held her breath.

She didn't think the dogs would kill a person - Ethan wouldn't allow them to do that. Would he?

Retro's timing was off by half a second. Burns got there first and jumped off the bank into the road, just as the man realized that he might be in trouble.

Another instant, and Burns was lunging with his front feet planted on the guy's chest. They both went down. Quinn didn't know if the dogs were that fast, or if the guy's actions were that slow, but by the time Retro got there, Burns was standing on top of Abel's chest and growling at his throat.

Abel tried to push the dog off, and Retro ducked in to snap at his hands. Abel pulled back with a yelp. "Get them off me!" he screeched. "Lady! Get them away!"

Quinn didn't answer. She took a step closer - not so close that he could get a good look at her. "I said, I think it's time for you to head on home, Mr. Welch. Isn't that right?"

Welch launched into a coughing fit. Good. She took the time to breathe in and steady her voice again. "Retro, Burns. Come."

The dogs looked up at the sound of their names, then Burns jumped over the man in the road and trotted her way. Retro looked back, then followed, like he was disappointed that he hadn't gotten in on the action. When they got to her, she put her free hand down to touch the tops of their heads. A small thank you. "I believe you'll be heading home now, Mr. Welch."

He was trying to scramble to his feet, but apparently drink made him dizzy when he actually tried to move. He sat down hard in the gravel with a grunt.

That was OK. Now that the dogs were with her, she could wait. She knew they would protect her.

Her hands were shaking. Maybe with cold, maybe with adrenaline, she wasn't sure which. All she knew was that she wanted Ethan to come home. She wanted to go into the house and take a hot shower and drink some tea. She wanted to feel safe. The day had seemed a week long, and she was ready for it to be over.

But there was no sign of Ethan, and at this point she was pretty sure that something had happened to him.

A new thought crept in, then burst fresh to the front of her mind. Did Abel have something to do with Ethan? On the same day Ethan disappeared, Abel showed up. Surely there had to be a connection.

Or did there? She knew herself well – she was prone to seeing patterns where there were none. It was part of her therapy, back in the city. It was entirely possible that two things like this could happen without being connected in any way. Right?

Or had Abel Welch hurt Ethan? Was this whole mess his fault? Ethan could no doubt hold his own in a fight with this...this...mossyhead, but what if Abel Welch had used that gun? What if he had ambushed Ethan in the woods and, well...

Her breath was coming in short quick gasps, thinking about it. She pushed the thought away.

Why would he? What reason would he have? It made no sense. None. She felt her heartbeat slow, just a little.

When Abel Welch finally made it to his feet, he startled her by screaming, "Those dogs are a menace, lady. They need to be put down."

She steadied herself. "Don't think so, Mr. Welch. You, maybe. Not them." Then she allowed herself a little grin. That was possibly the bravest thing she ever said in her life.

"I'll be calling the law."

"You do that. When you get home." He had no intention of calling the police, and she knew it. God only knew what they were doing down in that hollow, but she doubted they would want the cops poking around. "In fact, if you don't hurry up, I might just call the cops myself."

Like the gun, he wouldn't know if she had a cell phone or not. He probably didn't know that even if she'd grabbed her phone, there was no service back on this mountain. That was why she seldom carried it anywhere since she'd moved here. There was no point, and she had gotten out of the habit.

Not wanting to see his struggle to right himself, she had trained the flashlight's beam on the ground between them. Now she heard the clatter of gravel on his boots and pulled it up again. He was standing now, half turned back toward the road. Like he was about to leave, but still thinking about it. Finally, he started down the hill, back the way he had come. She hoped he got there safely and called it a night.

"Come on, boys. Let's go home," she said, touching each dog's head again. They started off across the field, Retro plowing ahead. Burns stayed closer to her, which she appreciated. She kept a hand on his collar all the way to the edge of the road, then stopped.

Abel was heading home, not looking back her way. Good. Maybe he would forget all about this and sleep it off, never to bother her again. Or maybe not, and that was OK, too. She now knew that she could handle him if he showed up again, and that was enough to quell the last of her fear. She kept an eye on him until he was completely out of sight, around the sharp turn that led back down to where he came from. Only then did she feel it was all right to relax.

She made it back to the porch without seeing him again, but still she stood there in the cold, not quite willing to go into the house yet. Instead, she shoved her hands into her pockets and looked around the property. The wind was picking up, and it was starting to snow again. She shivered.

She wished she knew where Ethan was, and why he wasn't home with her.

The dogs had taken off again, and she thought she should put them away in their pen before she went inside. If Ethan was out there in the woods - and where else could he be - and hurt, he could be very sick, or even dead, by morning. Even a healthy man was at risk in this kind of weather. It was full dark now.

Instead of sending the dogs to their pen, she called them to her and let them into the house. They were huge, snuffling at everything because they normally weren't allowed inside. The cabin was spacious for just her and Ethan, but two big dogs seemed to take up all the extra room. She tripped over them twice, just getting her coat off and drawing a bowl of water for them. Big mutts.

Once they were settled in front of the fireplace, lolling happily, she did what she should have done hours ago. She went to the phone to call nine-one-one.

With her luck, Ethan would come strolling in ten minutes after she called, grinning about wherever he'd been and wondering why she was so upset. He was like that, always happy on the surface of things. She was maybe the only person who knew he felt deeply about certain subjects, and she knew instinctively when to ask and when to let him be. Ethan could read her just as easily, too. Maybe twenty-five years of marriage really had made them clairvoyant.

Shaking her head, she grabbed the cordless phone from its cradle and took it to the fireplace, where she sat down between the dogs. Absent her husband, the dogs were good company. Leaning against Retro's side, she dialed the numbers and put the phone up to her ear.

There was silence on the other end while the call connected. This far out, it always took a moment or two.

But when nothing happened after a few more seconds, she pulled the phone away and looked at it. Yes, she had dialed the right number.

She clicked the phone off and then back on, then listened for a dial tone.

Nothing. The phone was out. She stared at it for a minute and tried again. Still nothing but silence.

Her world shrank. A lot. The dark outside got darker, the snow blew harder against the windows. Quinn took a deep breath and closed her eyes against the sinking feeling that threatened to take her down. Retro whined beside her, sensing her distress. She put a hand on his head, but barely felt the fur against her palm.

What the hell was she going to do now?

She should leave. Just...pack the dogs into the car and get out of here.

That, she knew, was the overreaction of the year.

First of all, the road leading in would be icy now that the sun was down. Second, that same road was treacherous, even in muddy weather. Carved into the side of a cliff, it was steep hillside to the left and a sharp, eighty-foot drop to her right. Third, she might be able to get out of here, and she would try if she had to, but she didn't like driving in the rain, much less the snow. If there was even a light dusting, she would either stay home or ask Ethan to drive her.

Now, of course, she saw the error in that. She should have been practicing - for the day that Ethan wasn't here. Today. She tossed the phone onto the sofa and stood up. Anger ripped through her. Where in the hell was he? Why wasn't he here to help her? Protect her? That was his job. He had promised.

He had promised.

Chapter Six

S he swallowed sudden tears and put the phone back on the hook. Walked over to lock the doors, then paused. The dogs would need to go out again if she was going to keep them inside with her.

She opened the door and called to them, then walked out onto the porch, watching as they took off into the yard. They probably thought she wanted another walk.

She was still wearing her coat, but it didn't do much against the wind, so she shoved her hands into her pockets.

That was when she noticed the dogs. They were both on alert, standing stiff at the bottom of the stairs. She followed their line of vision, expecting to see Abel Welch again, but there was nothing there. Only the fields off to the right of the house. The gate that led to another part of the property. The cedars.

After a moment, she saw something move. Light-colored, low to the ground. Under the cedar trees. Burns growled and shifted his weight, but neither of the dogs moved from their spot.

She looked again, but the darkness kept her from making out what they saw. The light-colored thing moved. Well, jerked, actually. Whatever it was, it was quick. She started that way, but paused at the top step and went back into the house.

On the top shelf of the bookcase was Ethan's handgun. She didn't know what kind - she only knew that he kept it loaded. He'd shown her how to take the safety off and cock the gun. He said that was all she needed to know.

She held it tightly in her right hand and went back outside. If Abel was out there, she was prepared.

But this wasn't Abel, she was almost sure of it. She made her way slowly down the stairs and passed the dogs. They hadn't moved and they were still staring hard into the trees.

"Retro," she said. "Come."

She didn't tell Burns to stay, so he would come too. "With me."

They moved to either side of her, which made her feel a million times better. She walked to the end of the porch and stopped there. "Hello?" she called for the second time this evening. "Anybody there?"

Nothing. No answer. No flash of a face looking her way. Just trees and shadows, moving.

It had to be an animal. Had to be. But what kind of animal? She'd never seen a deer move like this, and as far as she knew there weren't any stray dogs around.

But...coyotes.

She gripped the gun harder. It was cold and heavy in her hands.

Coyotes. They normally gave the farm a wide berth, because of the dogs and because Ethan spent so much time outside, around the house, but if they were hungry enough, desperate enough, they might come in close. Other folks on the mountain had confirmed it - lost cats, small mammal carcasses laying in the woods. It had been a long winter.

Burns growled again, and his pace had become more of a slinking. Odd, for him. Quinn wasn't sure what to make of it, but she kept walking.

About a hundred feet from the trees, she pulled the Mag Lite from her pocket and clicked it on. She caught a glimpse of ear, of tail. The coyotes finally noticed her and stopped what they were doing.

And what *were* they doing? She still couldn't see.

She started that way, but as she got closer, her steps slowed and eventually stopped. She didn't know why, beyond a bitter, nervous feeling in the pit of her gut. But that didn't make sense, because she'd only had this reaction once before...when she was ten.

It was her birthday that day, and her mother, in the middle of slathering pink icing on her birthday cake, had told her to go get her baby brother out of his crib. The party would be starting soon. Quinn was glad to do it - she loved little Tal, and didn't find him annoying at all even though her best friend Chrissy said she was supposed to. She planned on being the best big sister ever.

But halfway down the hall, her steps had faltered, just like now. Her belly had clenched tight, just like now. She remembered hoping that she wasn't getting a tummy ache, because then she wouldn't be able to enjoy her cake and ice cream. In fact, she decided that even if she was sick, she wouldn't tell her mother until after the party, when her friends were gone and the goodies were eaten.

Her mother found her there, standing in the hallway, somehow physically unable to go into her baby brother Tal's room.

There had been no birthday party that day. There had been no cake or ice cream or best friends. There had only been that long, low scream coming from her mother's throat, and then the ambulance ride, and then a funeral. Quinn refused to have a birthday party ever again, and thankfully Ethan understood. That was also the day she decided that all happy moments had a Catch.

Beside her, Burns barked, a sharp sound that ripped through her thoughts and made her jump. The coyotes looked up - three of them, that she could see - and Burns took off. They scattered away from the light and the impending teeth.

Burns," she called. He paused, mid-step, but didn't take his eyes off the spot where the coyotes had been. Her gut wrenched tighter.

Tonight, there was nobody to go over there for her. There was no mother to find the Catch and take care of the details. There was only her, Quinn, alone in the dark with two dogs and a fear that she couldn't place.

The trees were far enough from the house that she didn't really notice them unless she meant to, and even then it was usually just a glance in that direction. Ethan was the one who loved them and named them and patted them like they were friends.

The wind caught a few strands of her hair and blew them into her face. She scraped them away, took a deep breath, and forced herself to take a step. It was a horrible feeling, just like before. Like she was about to step out of an airplane, or off a tall bridge. Every nerve ending in her body felt raw, every brain cell screamed for her to stop.

But she couldn't stop. She couldn't just walk away and not see.

That was it - the seeing. She didn't want to, but she was the only one. There was no one else to do this for her.

She had to go.

Burns barked again. He was staring toward the darker woods beyond. She glanced in his direction and didn't see anything, but she knew that the coyotes hadn't gone far. If she went inside now, like she so desperately wanted to, they would come back.

But...come back to what?

The Catch. It loomed there, dark in the back of her mind. That didn't make sense, because she had taken great pains to make sure she could always see the Catch coming, couldn't she? She kept an eye out for it. She had designed her whole life - the right man, the right career, the proper amount of precaution - to avoid tragedy. So it couldn't be that, right?

The gut feeling crawled up into her throat. She choked out a small sob. Retro nuzzled her hand.

She forced her legs to move.

The thin lights from the yard didn't reach quite this far, so the long shadows of the cedars blended into the woods beyond. For all she knew, there was a ten story monster behind those cedars, ready to eat her alive. The wind howled through the thin trees as she approached, bending the tops and making the thick, sharp needles shudder. She shivered too, cold beyond belief.

Burns was sniffing around the bottom of the trees. She didn't know why, but she didn't want him over there. "Stop it. Burns, come."

He looked up, looked back at what he was sniffing, and reluctantly trotted her way through the falling snow.

She gripped the flashlight and strode forward a few steps, both dogs by her side again. The flashlight beam juttered with every step and her inner distress threatened to halt her in her tracks, but she didn't dare think about it and she didn't dare stop. If she did, she would never start again.

It was no more than a couple of hundred paces to the cedars, but each one felt like it took an hour. The snow was piling up so that she kicked it out in front of her with her toes. It fell and made speckles ahead, like it was showing her the way.

She knew the way - she just didn't want to go.

Her flashlight caught a hint of yellow, and another sob jerked from her throat. Her feet tried to drag again. If she didn't go forward, she could pretend like she didn't know. Like Schrodinger's cedars. Right?

When she got to him, and yes, she'd known it was him from the moment she started walking this way, hadn't she? She'd known that one mystery, at least, would be resolved at the end of her walk through this storm. The cedars bowed, as if in greeting, too happy for the tragedy they protected. When she got to him, she fell to her knees, blind with grief.

Chapter Seven

She didn't hear the sob that came out of her throat. She felt it, a raw, ripping heat that exploded from her as she reached out to touch him. She almost did, almost brushed the hand that she had clutched so many times. But then she pulled back, unsure.

His face - what was left of it - was as pale as the snow covering his lap and feet. The darkness of his hair and brows stood out starkly, yet even they were frosted over. She fought the urge to brush the ice from his face. His clothes were glossy with ice. Red ice, like frozen wine. Part of his head was gone. One blue eye stared back at her, plaintive and still. Empty.

She could see his yellow jacket flung open and puckered. The coyotes had done that, probably. They would want to drag him away from the house, away from the dogs and the lights. She had interrupted them. Thank God.

Retro whined beside her, but she barely heard him. She was breaking inside, cracking apart. Her ears were ringing. The Catch had come, and like before, it was beyond her ability to understand right now.

"Ethan." His name burst harshly from her parted lips. Then, more softly, "Oh, Ethan."

Still afraid to touch him, she reached out and touched his coat. Or meant to, but her hand brushed freezing steel. Shining the light, she saw the rifle for the first time. It lay against his far shoulder, the butt cradled against one leg.

He had done this. She was sure of it. "Why, Ethan? Why would you do such a thing?" she asked, as if he had done some silly thing, like buying a new truck or forgetting to feed the dogs. Her world slid away from her. Her voice was tinny and hollow and sounded far away.

The darkness sparkled and her head spun. She was going to faint.

Beside her, Retro barked.

She jumped, and realized that her jeans were soaking through and her hair was wet. She was freezing, and when she touched her face her tears were icy. She needed to get inside. She needed to call for help.

But she couldn't. The phone was out. What was she going to do? He was too big for her to carry, she knew that without even thinking about it. She crawled away from him, got up out of the snow, and ran back toward the house. The warm lights. The living room where he was supposed to be. And as she ran, she screamed at the dark sky.

She slammed in through the door and landed on her side in the floor, with Retro close behind her. Burns was outside, left behind when she shut the door, but she couldn't care right now. She wasn't capable. He would be fine.

She realized that she was gasping for breath, sucking in huge gulps of warm air. Her body was running on automatic, trying to warm up, trying to make all systems go again. It didn't realize that the Catch was finally happening, and that she didn't want to breathe, or feel, or move, or exist. Ethan was gone, and she was dumped dead on the floor. She didn't think she would ever get up.

The gasps warmed her lungs eventually, and then she began to cry. He was out there, in the dark. So cold. He must be cold. She wanted to hear him stomping snow across the porch and then come in laughing about something the dogs did. She wanted him to give her a kiss on top of the head and ask, "What's for dinner?"

He would never do those things again. He would never lift her off the ATV and tell her to walk because her puns made him groan. He would never grin at her over someone's insistence that the CIA killed John Kennedy. He would never smack her on the butt or kiss her or fold her into his lap on a cold winter night like this one.

She would never be warm again.

Outside the door, she heard a rumble. Burns. Growling.

The coyotes were back.

She would have given anything to pretend like the last hour hadn't happened. It was impossible. It was wrong. Some nightmare that she couldn't shake.

It was Ethan was out there, and she needed to bring him inside. Before...before. It was her turn to protect him, and she didn't know if she could do it.

The fire warmed her through her coat, and her mind floated. She thought about their wedding and their fights, yes, that all filtered through her mind. But then she thought about the way he always held her and kissed her before he left for work, or lately, the way he came in smelling of cold and fresh air, and the way he came home to her every evening and shared his day, asked about hers. They were a team, he always said.

Of course, he also always said that he was lucky to have her. What had changed?

People always said that a dying man's life flashed before his eyes, but that wasn't true. That life flashed through the mind of the person they left behind.

They were only just beginning this latest adventure. It was a brand new page, and he'd been excited about it. More excited than her - coming back to the land, like his family, had been his dream, not hers. They had liquidated everything back in Atlanta and brought it here, where they were supposed to live happily ever after.

Not...like this. Never like this.

She felt small and cold and lost, and she wasn't sure she could move, even if she wanted to, which she didn't.

Retro licked her hand, then nuzzled his nose in near her ear, making her shiver. She moaned and looked at him with one eye. The other was face down on the rug and she couldn't lift her head. "What happened, Retro?" she murmured. "What happened to him?"

Because Ethan loved life - the good and the bad and the weird, maybe especially the weird. So why had he stepped out, as they used to say? Why had he jumped ship, just as they were about to sail off into their sunset? She remembered sitting at their dining room table in the city, going over the finances, and calculating that they had approximately forty years left. Calculating if they could afford to retire early, and realizing that they could. Easily. The money was there, they had no kids to put through college, and why shouldn't they? Wasn't this what they'd worked for?

He had been thrilled with the idea, excited to show her the ways of the gentleman farmer. She had called him that - gentleman farmer - for a week afterward, until he threatened to call her Bessie if she did it again. He hadn't meant it, he never meant his teasing, and they had laughed at the idea of him running through Belk or Neiman Marcus bellowing "Bessie!" at the top of his lungs. Of course, it never happened.

And now the rest of it wasn't going to happen, either, was it? Because he was gone, with no hints and no goodbyes.

She reached an arm out and wrapped it around Retro's neck. Dragged him to her and buried her face into his bristling fur. He smelled like fresh air, snow, and dog. She cried some more, or she hadn't stopped. She wasn't sure, and it didn't matter. Nothing mattered.

She eventually pushed herself up from the floor and then dragged to her feet. Burns was still growling periodically from outside the front door, and she knew she had to take care of Ethan. She had to get Burns inside. She had to find a way to get help.

She didn't know how she was going to do any of those things, and by the time she got back to the front door, she put her head on the cold wood, exhausted.

Before she went out she tried the phone again. Still dead. She tossed it onto the sofa and went to the bedroom closet to get an old blanket. It was a yellow one with satin edging. She liked to curl up under it and read while Ethan watched TV, but she needed it now.

Then she left Retro by the fireplace and went to get Ethan. A sharp blast of snow and wind hit her in the face and stole her breath when she stepped outside. Snow was driving toward the ground now, tiny missiles of stinging ice. She gasped and held the blanket to her face to shield it for a moment. Burns danced around her feet, waiting to see what they were going to do next. He followed her down the stairs and across the yard.

Less in shock now, she bent down to look at Ethan again. It wasn't any easier, but this time she saw more detail. He was wearing a toboggan, but it was almost unrecognizable now. It had once been a jaunty hunter's orange, but now was soaked with the red of his drained life. The right side of his head was destroyed, and what was left was ragged and black. She saw that his jacket was zipped all the way up. Had he been cold when he died? She hoped not - no one deserved that.

His hands had fallen away from the rifle. The right one, which was closer to her, was flung out to the side. His hand lay curled in the snow. She should have been able to see it from the house, but then again, maybe one of the coyotes had tugged it out that way. His left hand was laying on his belly, like he had a simple stomach bug and would be all right in a minute or two.

She looked away for a moment. Then she stood up and took the time to spread out the blanket as close to him as she could.

She wanted nothing more than to go back into the house and pretend that none of this was happening. She wanted to yell at him to get up, that he was scaring her, and this wasn't funny. She could do those things, but none of it would matter.

She swallowed a sob and went back to work. She took the out-flung arm and gently tugged it. His body tipped to the side a little, but not enough. It was because his legs were crossed - his knees blocked a smooth transition from sitting to laying. She went around and straightened them. First one and then the other. They were stiff, from cold or death she couldn't tell. She brushed the snow from his jeans.

His toboggan had shifted a little with the movement, showing more damage underneath, but she made sure to keep her eyes averted. There was nothing she could do about it - no cleaning, bandaging or praying would help Ethan now. Deep down, there was also the thought – if you don't look, it isn't real.

The idea had been to lay him onto the blanket, wrap him up, and pull him to the house. That wouldn't work now, because of the way he'd fallen. Touching him as gingerly as she could, she got her hands under his arms and, inch by inch, shifted him to where she needed his weight to be. She was holding her breath again, and sobbing again, but she ignored all of that, turned off her head and heart, and did the work that needed doing. He was stiff. And cold, so cold.

He was heavy enough that she almost couldn't do it. It took a lot of strength, inch by inch, to get him completely onto the blanket. Burns stood by, watching the woods where the coyotes had gone. Once in a while he let out a little whine, and she would say something to soothe him, but afterward she couldn't remember what. Later, all she could remember was the feel of Ethan's lifeless body against her hands, and she would have nightmares about this for months.

By the time she got Ethan situated on the blanket and his rifle laying alongside his arm, pointing away, her hands and feet were numb and her hair was a wet mess in her eyes and plastered to her cheeks. She'd lost the ponytail somewhere along the way.

She gripped the edge of the blanket, but she couldn't feel it. When she tightened her grip, the satin edging slicked out of her hands. When she tried again it tore away. Just an inch, but she had to completely change her grasp. She got hold of the corners, twisted them around her hands and began to pull.

The way she held the blanket raised Ethan's head from the ground, but the rest of him seemed to fight her, as if he didn't want to come inside. "I don't want you to come inside, either," she told him, feeling a tick of anger through her fear and shock. "But you'll get eaten by something if I leave you out here."

It was true - the thought of sharing the house with her husband's dead body in the next room made her skin crawl. Yes, she had loved him, and yes, he was dead. She still didn't like the idea. In normal circumstances, she supposed that an ambulance would take him away, and she would come later to identify him and make arrangements. In these circumstances? These terrifying, dismal circumstances?

Well, she was doing the best she could.

It felt to her tired, shaking muscles that every bump of uneven ground caught his body's angles. She had to fight for each foot of progress, wrestle with every hump and rock. His heels left deep furrows in the rough snow, marking her effort. The snow piled up ahead of the blanket where his shoulders widened so that she was forced to stop and clear it out of the way every couple of feet. The entire time, with Burns's help, she kept an eye on the road and the tree, looking for either coyotes or the return of Abel Welch.

Every few feet, she tripped under the weight of her load and fell to her knees. She would struggle upright again and keep going. She was certain that this awful journey would never end, that she was condemned to pull her husband across the snow for eternity. It felt like hours before she got to the driveway and cut across it toward the house. It felt like weeks until she was within range of the outdoor lights. And then the yard began its slow slope upward, making her struggle even harder. The whole time, she wanted to look away from the bone and black of Ethan's destroyed head, but she had to make sure he didn't bump off the blanket. She didn't have the ability to pick him up again.

Burns stayed close, but every so often he would circle out and check the area around her, as if he knew to play bodyguard. Meanwhile Retro, finally realizing he'd been left behind, scratched at the wood door, sending her nerves into overdrive every time she heard the clawing on wood. It made her want to hurry before he did too much damage, but of course she couldn't hurry. Ethan was heavy, the ground beneath him was uncooperative, and she was nearing the point of collapse. Also, she couldn't begin to care about the stupid door.

At this point it would be easier for her to go get a shovel and bury him here, than to get him back to the house - and she still wasn't sure how she was going to get him up the stairs.

The people who owned the house before - an elderly couple who went to live with their children, had planted the strangest arrangement of flowerbeds that Quinn had ever seen. Ethan had joked that they were creating a pinball effect, and that every flowerbed in some random spot was the bumpers they used to get them to the car in the driveway. She could almost agree - the beds were all different shapes and bordered by whatever happened to be handy - bricks, rubber piping, wood planks, and even a set of tires cut in arcs to look like black, knobby rainbows. Worse, they were all over the place - one five feet from the corner of the porch, another right in front of the concrete parking area, still another a foot from the walkway. There was no rhyme or reason for the way the yard was laid out, and one of the first things Ethan had done when he caught a warm day was transplant everything and remove all those silly borders, leaving the ground to resettle into a proper lawn.

The whole operation left small indentations in the grass here and there, wherever the beds had been. It was one of these that she fell into, backwards, smacking her head sharply on a small stone. She'd been pulling so hard that she wasn't able to catch herself.

For a moment she just lay there in the snow. Her head spun and she considered just passing out right there, giving up and joining Ethan in whatever afterlife he'd found. She was wet, cold, and so tired that she couldn't think straight. But the rock hadn't even cut her, and after a moment or two her vision cleared, so she forced herself up and kept going.

By the time she got to the steps she was sweating, which made it worse when she bent over and the wind blew up the tail of her coat. She moaned in pure misery every single time and thought about going inside to warm herself in front of the fire.

There were only three steps, but they were steep. She stopped and sat down on the bottom one, near Ethan's head, and brushed the accumulated snow gently from the good side of his face. After that, she decided that she couldn't look at him anymore or she *would* give up.

She gave up the fight and went inside to bake in front of the fire before beginning the next round. This time, Burns shoved past her before she even got the door fully open. Retro was of course standing on the other side, so she had to step over the tangle of dogs before she was able to feel the warmth of proper shelter.

Her heart ached more than her body. She sank to her knees in front of the fire and let the flames warm her hands and face for a few moments. Then she turned her mind to getting Ethan inside. She didn't think she could lift him, even one step at a time. He would just slide back down when she moved him from step to step, and she would have to start over again and again.

She didn't think she had the fortitude for that, no matter how much she loved Ethan. She already felt ashamed of her earlier anger with him, but she was also exhausted.

At least the logistics of it all kept her panic at bay. When this was done, she didn't know what would happen to her mind.

Once she was warm, she let herself out the back door and went to the barn, looking around for anything that might give her an idea. She thought she remembered Ethan coming home with new rope last week sometime. She wondered where he had put it. Flipping on the bare light bulbs that hung from the ceiling, she saw that the tractor had a winch. She didn't know how to use it, though. She stood and stared at several tangled, oily ropes and pulleys, but she didn't know if she could rig up anything that might help her. The wall to her left was lined with useless tools. What was she going to do with a crowbar or a garden rake?

Farther back, in the partition that held the small tractor, she found something that might work. It was a full sheet of plywood. If she could brace it at the bottom and slide Ethan up to the porch with the rope, if she found it, she might be able to manage. Looking at the broad sheet of yellow wood, her failing muscles ached even worse. She wanted to give up.

Behind her, from the door she just came through, a voice said, "Whatcha doin'?"

Chapter Eight

Quinn spun around, almost tripping over a big bag of deer feed, and gasped. She caught herself with one hand against the rough wood wall.

Abel Welch was back, and the grin on his face wasn't exactly friendly. He blocked the door.

Only then did she realize that the dogs had been barking in the house. She'd been too busy thinking to pay attention.

"What are you doing here?" she asked, her voice sharp in the cold air. He looked drunker than before, if that were possible. He also looked mean. Suddenly everything about her surroundings stood out in sharp relief - the dust floating in the dim bulb light, the smell of hay and sweet feed, the mustiness of old hay, and the shadows that filled every corner of the small stall. The wood of the barn popped and cracked in the freezing air.

He came inside, his steps heavy and shuffling. She stepped back the same distance, reeling from the alcohol on his breath and clothes.

Immediately she knew that was a bad idea - men like Abel could smell fear a mile away, and the way his eyes lit up, he was no exception. Her mind went to the contents of the barn behind her - what could she use as a weapon? Because the booze would make him brave, wouldn't it? Because she was completely alone right now, and he knew it. If he was here, he had to walk right past Ethan's body, so of course he knew.

She thought about Ethan, thought about the rifle laying by his side, and wished she had it here with her.

But she didn't, and a bag of corn wasn't going to get her out of this. Neither was the tractor, or a sheet of plywood, or locking herself in a stall, although she considered that one for a few moments. She just didn't think she could get past him to do it.

Then she remembered the crowbar. It was hanging on the other side of the barn, and she would have to work her way around the tractor to get to it. She thought that maybe she was faster that Abel Welch, and definitely more sure of her footing. If he had to run he'd most likely fall flat on his face.

That would be funny, if he didn't mean her harm.

But he did - she could tell by the way his body leaned in toward her, the way his glazed eyes followed her every move. The way he was practically licking his lips and looking her up and down like she was more dinner than human.

So she could outrun him well enough, and she could get to the crowbar. But she would still be trapped in here with him unless he fell on his face. It could happen, but she wasn't about to count on it.

Before she did anything, she needed to get her heartbeat under control. Right now, it was pumping so hard that she was dizzy, and that was no help at all. Her muscles were tightening up. She didn't dare even blink. As she looked at him, she let a tiny movie play out in her head. It was a trick her old therapist taught her as a way to ward off a coming panic attack. It was a ridiculous movie - one where she was able to jump on top of the tractor, kick him hard enough to take him down, jump over him and run out the door. Back to the house where the guns were. Then she could hold him hostage until the authorities arrived, which might be...when? Never? In the spring?

She shook the movie away, but it had served its purpose - she felt a little calmer now. Not that she could do those things, but she could do something.

She moved a step or two toward the tractor. "You need to leave."

Abel didn't answer. He shuffled forward a step or two, keeping his eyes on her. He snorted, then he sneezed.

Frantic laughter caught in her throat, just because this entire situation was absurd. She was trapped in the dark with a guy who might be taken down by allergies. If she had known he was going to do that, she would have made her move then. As it was, he recovered fairly quickly and came even closer, until he was leaning on the big steel grill of the tractor. She was beside the rear tire. That left only the tall fender and the long nose between them. She needed to back up and get over the brush hog, which was a six-foot square mower hitched to the back of the tractor. She stood very still, trying to decide when to move.

She didn't dare look at the wall, where the crowbar hung. That would give her away. She'd never known many angry or dangerous drunks. Most of the people she knew didn't get drunk, and the ones that did tended to simply talk too much. She and Ethan weren't regular drinkers, either. Ethan only drank on special occasions, and she couldn't remember the last time she'd had a drink at all. For all she knew Abel here was getting ready to pass out.

Except that would be too easy, and nothing about this night was easy. Her husband was dead in the front yard, the dogs were in the house, and now this moron was trying to cause trouble when she could least afford it.

Her anger at Ethan bloomed again, but this time she focused it on Abel Welch's forehead.

Of all the people who had to die today, God had picked the wrong one. Why couldn't this man have fallen into the river and drowned, instead of coming here and threatening her. "Get the fuck out of here!" she yelled.

His nostrils flared, but he cocked an amused half-grin. "I don't think I need to do that."

She pivoted on her left foot and turned toward the rear of the tractor. She needed to hop over the hitch - it was about knee high, but lots of pins and bolts stuck out in several directions.

Of course she caught her pants leg on one. Of course she did. She cussed again as she went down on one knee, narrowly missing one of those pins with her eye. Only a quick hand stopped her from getting seriously hurt. She reached for her pants leg, but the pin had punched through it. She jerked and heard a rip, and then Abel was around the front of the tractor and grabbing at her.

He could only half stand up, and under less insane circumstances she would have admired his determination. As it was, she jerked at her pants again and used her free hand against his chest, trying to push him back. He loomed over her and knelt down, bending her wrist the wrong way.

From this distance she could see every black pore on his face and every wiry hair on his head. He reeked of booze and body odor. She gagged.

Her pants leg ripped free, finally, but now she had to finish scrambling over the hitch without getting caught again. She gave the sneering man a hard shove and dove for it. Her belly scraped hard across the frozen steel, and she nearly landed on her head, but she was across. Abel was coming over now, too, grunting about it but close behind her.

She got to her feet, belly still burning, and reached up. Her fingers scrambled, found the nail, the wood beam and then the crowbar that hung there. She grabbed it.

It was a big one. To her abused muscles it felt like it weighed a hundred pounds, but she knew better. Ethan had been teasing her for a couple of months now about getting in shape for all the farm work ahead of them, and she had laughed it off. Now, if she could have a do-over, she would have started working out years ago.

She wrapped her hands around the crowbar and hefted it. Cold steel burned her palms. She took aim at Abel's head, but then hesitated. Stupid. She realized that she was crying again.

This was gross, and her stomach turned at the thought of using the tool against hard bone and sallow flesh. She didn't want to kill anybody, and this crowbar could easily cave in a skull. Was it worth it, even if her life was on the line?

In that instant, he looked up at her and grinned. His eyes lit up when he realized that she had stopped running. He didn't notice that she couldn't have run if she wanted to, that effectively she was cornered.

She gritted her teeth, closed her eyes, and brought the crowbar down across the side of Abel's head. She pulled her strength at the last minute - he was just a drunk, he didn't deserve to die over this, her mind kept repeating. She just needed to stop him. The crowbar landed hard enough, even so. She let out a little scream when she did it, and thought for sure that she was going to puke all over herself. A muffled thud reached her ears, and the metal vibrated back through to her hands and forearms, making them sting so much that she almost dropped the thing. The crowbar caught and ripped at his head, then glanced off near his ear. Blood poured down onto his cheek. The tool's momentum spun her sideways.

She tightened up and held onto it, just in case. In case she didn't do the damage she imagined, in case the damage didn't stop Abel Welch. Hadn't she read somewhere that drunk people didn't get hurt the way -?

She watched him slump over the hitch like an old rug, his filthy, sweat-soaked shirt pulling tight enough to keep him from falling over onto his head.

The side of his skull was already swelling, and she thought she heard him groan a little, but she didn't wait around to find out. She dropped the crowbar, grabbed the tractor's steering wheel and pulled herself up and over, dropping to the other side on wobbly knees. Then she ran for the house, still fighting nausea.

She was on the porch, pushing open the door, when she heard his struggling, rasping voice yell, "Hey! Hey, you!"

She let out a scream and slammed the door behind her.

Locks. She needed to lock everything. The back door had two - the regular knob lock and the dead bolt. The front door had four - two deadbolts for good measure and a slider over the regular lock. She was sucking in air, tripping over the dogs, and sobbing, hard enough that her chest hurt.

But then she could stop - the dogs were here, the guns were here, and there was no noise from Abel outside.

She sank to the floor in front of the fireplace and let the dogs press against her. Their bodies warmed her and their rough doggy kisses were a comfort. Ethan was still out there, but she couldn't do anything about that right now, no matter how guilty she felt about it. She just had to hope that the smell of Abel would keep away the coyotes and any other scavenging critters.

Low thumps made her squeak again. Burns and Retro both turned and growled at the back door. Their fur rose high on their backs. Burns took a step in that direction, but she tucked her fingers into his collar to hold him there with her. She didn't want him to step away.

All three of them jumped when Abel yelled, "Hey, bitch!" and pounded hard on the door. Boom, boom. Twice. Then silence.

She held her breath and tried to listen.

The silence was almost worse than the noise, because it meant she didn't know where he was, or what he might be doing. She would have thought that a crowbar would have knocked him out for longer, but apparently that article about drunks was true.

She got up and ran to yank the curtains in the room closed. At every window, she took the half-second to check the lock - a small half-moon shaped contraption that closed easily. The dogs stayed right with her, even though she was only moving a few feet at a time. She practically waded through them to get from window to window, stressing her tired muscles that much more.

She thought about him shooting through the glass, and realized that he had come after her with both hands. Where had his gun gone? Had he ever had one? Her mind reeled unable to remember. Hadn't he been aiming the gun at the dog? Had her eyes tricked her? Maybe he had a gun and lost it. As long as he wasn't armed, she had a chance.

The cabin was well-built, but no structure could keep a man out if he really wanted to come inside. There was always a way. It was her job to think faster than Abel and bar those ways.

Reflexively, she snatched up the phone as she made her way past the sofa and tried for a dial tone, but it was still sickeningly dead. How could she -.

The lights went out. One of the dogs whined. The light on the phone in her hand went out.

Quinn froze. Her skin tingled and she swallowed a whimper. She sucked in a very quiet, very deep breath, then let it out. "OK," she whispered. "OK. Now what?"

Had the storm snapped a line somewhere? It happened fairly often here, once a week if the weather was particularly bad. The electric company usually came and fixed it within a couple of hours. That could mean help was on the way.

Or had Abel cut the lights somehow?

She started to panic, but then forced it back. First things first.

The breaker box was in the master bedroom, behind the door. "Retro," she half-whispered. He snuffled and came to bump against her leg. She took his collar and half led, half leaned on him to get to the bedroom. She found the little latch and clicked it open. She shielded the flashlight with her hand and aimed it at the breakers. They were all lined up, just as they should be, so it wasn't a simple trip.

That narrowed things down a little. Either the electric went out as it usually did, or Abel was messing with the box outside. She somehow doubted that he was that smart, or that brave. He was just a drunk. Right?

If it wasn't Abel that was good news. She just needed to keep him out, then watch for the electric truck, and she was saved.

She clicked the breaker box closed again and walked around the bed to lock that window and close the curtains.

A soft thump from somewhere near the other end of the house startled her. Retro let out a gruff bark. On the other end of the house, Burns went crazy, barking and digging at the front door. She could hear his claws making mincemeat of the wood.

She started to call out to him, then realized that if she did, Abel would know her exact location in the house. Instead, she let out a whistle.

She heard him stop digging, heard his claws on the kitchen floor as he made his way to her. He was still growling, but he came.

Something heavy hit the front door. Quinn bit the inside of her lip and listened.

All of this uncertainty was wearing at her nerves. She was aching with sustained tension and her stomach roiled with worry. She needed help, and there was no way to get it.

She went to the bed and sat down, staring at nothing while she tried to think. What could she do right here and right now to solve this problem?

A million things went through her mind, and most of them were ridiculous. She could offer Abel money to go away - guys like that loved money - but she doubted that would work right now. He wanted something else. She could scream at him, shoot at him, or set the dogs on him....

Wait a minute. Burns was ready to tear the guy limb from limb - why didn't she let him? That's why they bought the dogs, wasn't it?

But if Burns got hurt, she'd feel guilty for the rest of her life.

Then again, if Abel got in here, her life wouldn't be very long, would it? She remembered something that Ethan had told her once. It had been a beautiful day in December, cold but sunny. She'd been sitting on the porch, watching Ethan work with Retro. He would give a variety of commands in rapid fire fashion, and the dog jumped into action, reacting and moving and doing everything he was told. He was all quick and precise, like a well-designed machine. When it was over Ethan, his cheeks red but bunched into a grin, had given Quinn a delighted thumbs up. "I think he's got it," he yelled from the yard.

Later, when Ethan had given Retro his treats and penned him, he came up onto the porch to join Quinn.

"How does he respond so perfectly?" she asked, still in awe at the dog-plus-man show she'd just seen.

"He loves it." Ethan had taken her hand. "Did you see how excited he acted? Dogs are happiest when they're working. When they're doing what they are trained to do, and doing it well."

That had been a good day, the kind of day she would remember forever. Ethan had been right - Retro was never so happy as when he was doing something. Burns either. She didn't know why that was, but she had seen the truth of it that day, and every day she went to watch them work. They were at their happiest after a good, strong workout. Like true soldiers.

She sank to her knees and gave Burns a hug. His thick neck muscles were taut against her arms. He gave her an absent-minded lick on the ear, then went back to staring down the hall, toward the front door.

Should she let both dogs out?

No, she decided, almost without thinking about it. No. She would be terrified without one of them in here with her, and Burns was the more aggressive of the two. Ethan had always warned her against spoiling Retro too often, but she hadn't paid attention. Not that he wouldn't do the job, he was just more willing to be swayed with a treat or a chance to play.

"Burns," she whispered, running his soft ears through her fingers. The heat from his body felt good against her hands. "Buddy, I need you to work now, all right?

Burns whined, trying to divide his attention between her and the rest of the house.

"I need you to get rid of this guy. He's going to hurt us." She realized that she could be sending the dog into danger, but deep down, she hoped that the sight of those teeth would send Abel Welch running for his life.

Chapter Nine

Abel Welch didn't feel the cold. He barely felt the side of the house when he bounced off it to make his way around to the front door. The snow was breaking his stride, making him push through with every step. He cursed at it silently, but kept kicking it out of the way until he got to the front steps.

The man lying in the snow beside them gave him pause. He spent a good bit of time staring down at Ethan Galloway's body, waiting for him to get up. When he didn't, Abel spent more time trying to figure out if this was real at all. Maybe it was a decoy, as if she could scare him away with a toy.

He toed the head of the dead guy. It flopped over some, enough that Abel could see the damage done by the rifle.

Speaking of which...he bent to get a closer look. There was a rifle, laying just under the dead man's shoulder, as if he'd rolled on it in his sleep. Abel used his foot to roll the man's body and picked up the weapon. It was as real as the corpse He grinned at it and held it up to the small amount of light from the dusk to dawn in the yard.

Then he checked the chamber. It wasn't loaded. Dude had probably just brought enough bullets to off himself, and that was it.

That made him frown. He swayed a little and leaned against the side of the house, thinking. The snow blew into his face and he swiped it away impatiently.

What could he do with an empty rifle to get her out here?

It was then that another thought crossed his mind. What if the dead dude hadn't offed himself? What if little miss crowbar in there did it? What if she was on her way to bury him when Abel interrupted her?

It didn't really matter, he supposed. The rifle was out here with him now, wasn't it? That brought the grin back for a second, until he realized that a home with a gun usually had several more stashed away. It would be good to assume that she was armed in there.

So why hadn't she shot him yet? She had all the advantages - sight, sound, time to aim. What was stopping her, other than that most important of all the facts - women were pussies?

He chuckled at that, which made him sway so hard that he almost fell on top of the dead guy before he managed to catch himself with a hand on the siding.

Abel wasn't known for his suave abilities with the ladies. He wasn't actually known for much, to be honest, except small time in the local lock-up and a few dalliances with the wives of his friends. He came from the wrong side of everything - wrong neighborhood, wrong education, wrong upbringing. He didn't much care, either, as long as he had a roof over his head and some sweet whiskey to warm his bones. Thanks to Patty's stupid fool heart, he had both.

Rick had already tried to kick him out twice, but Patty, a nursing assistant at the senior home, had stepped in both times to stop that shit from happening. It was too cold, she'd told her husband, to let a man freeze. It didn't hurt for Abel to stay here.

Except that, yeah, it had hurt, hadn't it? Ricky-boy had tried this morning to kick old Abel out of the house, since Patty was off to work. But that hadn't been in the cards for Rick. No, sir. In fact, Abel had spilled Ricky-boy's whole deck. Now Patty's husband was probably tangled pretty well in the brush downriver, hidden pretty good. The current had swiped him right away. Easy as pie. It would be awhile before anybody found him.

At first, after he had used Ricky's own hunting knife to cut his throat, Abel had figured on waiting around for Patty. When she got home there'd most likely be hell to pay, but that was all right. His own wife Annabelle had tried that shit, and he'd shut her down, back in the day. It wasn't that hard - men were bigger and stronger for a reason, weren't they? Annabelle had run off to mama with three cracked ribs, two black eyes, and a swollen wrist, but she had run, and Abel really hadn't thought she was worth chasing.

Of course, mama was in Richmond, about three hundred miles away, so Patty wouldn't know this. Good thing, too, or her heart might have listened to Ricky's red flags. Now, Patty was the proud owner of fifteen river front acres and no husband. Abel had already decided – he would pat her on the back and help her mourn the loss, but then he'd take Rick's place. It was a good place, too. Patty didn't even make Ricky work. All in good time. Patty would see how it was meant to be, how much better Abel was than Rick. He was bigger, stronger, and more willing to protect what was his, for starters. Right now, he considered Patty, her house, and her land all his. There for the taking. He chuckled to himself, thinking how easy it was when a man was willing to do what it took.

In the end, she would thank him. He'd raise those boys right and raise the girl to be a proper woman. She would be proud of her kids when he was done with them.

But now this new opportunity had fallen into his lap, hadn't it? This woman didn't have kids to worry about, far as he could see. She didn't have a beat up old rustbucket in the driveway or - evidently - a husband to worry about. Abel glanced down at Ethan Galloway and snorted. Nope. This gal had taken care of the old man herself. That was the kind of woman Abel really needed.

And now he could have it, if he played his cards right.

Course, that would leave poor Patty all alone down there by the river, wouldn't it? A waste. Maybe Killer Lady up here on the mountain would be willing to share.

Maybe it didn't matter. He'd share if he damned well felt like it.

That got another chuckle out of Abel and this time when he started swaying, he sat down hard on the next-to-bottom step with a grunt. He laughed anyway. Life was suddenly looking pretty damned good from here.

In the middle of imagining his new status, Abel happened to glance down at the dead dude, and something occurred to him. Setting the rifle aside, he dropped off the step to his knees on the wet snow and started going through Ethan Galloway's pockets, a look of determined confusion on his face.

When he got to the blood-soaked front pocket of the dead man's jeans, the confusion cleared and the gruff grin came back. He pulled out a handful of shells and laughed out loud.

Chapter Ten

S he gave Burns a final kiss, stood up, and, holding tightly to his collar, tip-toed to the back door in the hall. Slowly, wincing at every little sound, she disabled the locks.

If she was right, Abel would still be at the front door, and he couldn't see her release the dog. A blast of freezing air hit her face when she peeked out. There was no sound or movement at the back of the house. The barn lights were still on, lighting up the snow with a warm yellow glow. It might have been festive under better circumstances, but right now it was just another threat. Less light meant that Abel couldn't see any movement, either.

It didn't matter - she certainly wasn't about to risk her life to turn out the barn lights.

She released Burns's collar and started to speak the word Ethan had trained n him so well. "Jump" was the command he had given them, and it was the one she knew Burns would respond to immediately.

But when she turned loose of his collar, no words were necessary. He was straining against her hold anyway, so when she opened the door he was gone before the word could leave her mouth. He jumped from the back porch - a drop of at least three feet, into two feet of snow. Only his head, tail and the top of his back were visible, and then he was gone, around the side of the house.

She slammed the door again, locked the locks, and listened for...anything,

The waiting, holding her breath, was as scary as the noise. What was Burns doing?

Something slammed against the front door and seemed to jar the whole house. Burns barked.

That set Retro off. He tore through the house to the front door before she could stop him. When she caught up, he was barking hard enough to crack his ribs, it seemed, and glaring at the front door. When he glanced back at her, the look in his eyes told her to hurry up, to open it, but she didn't dare. Not until she was sure Abel was out of commission.

She called Retro to her side and stood in the center of the dark living room, trying to think, but that was nearly impossible. All she could focus on was Burns and the growling, barking struggle going on outside. Something slammed against that end of the house. A curse rang through the air. She made out what sounded like scuffling - or scraping, as if something was being dragged across the porch floorboards. She cringed when a sharp scream cut the air.

Retro pressed against her leg, hard enough to knock her over if she didn't steady herself against Ethan's big recliner. He growled low in his throat, and the fur on his back was bristling under her palm. He wouldn't take his eyes off the front door, not even when she spoke his name.

Should she have let him out, too? Was she wrong to send Burns out alone? He was the stronger and more protective of the two, but was that enough? The nails of her free hand bit into her palms and her heartbeat thumped in her ears.

Good or bad, it was too late to call back the decision.

Think, Quinn. You need to think. What next? She started toward the window in the front, but then something slammed against the front door. Another bout of cursing and then she heard Abel yell her name.

She jumped, nearly biting her tongue. How had he known her name? She knew she hadn't given it to him. She doubted that his hosts even knew it, but she supposed that was possible. Had Ethan ever spoken to this man? Maybe ran across him in the woods? Maybe they chatted for a while, the way people around here did, even if they didn't know each other at all.

She'd always considered that dimension of small town life a little creepy, but Ethan considered it charming. Of course he would - he loved people and never met a stranger, as his dad said so often.

Well, she had, and this Abel character was stranger than most. It felt like he came out of nowhere, at the worst moment possible. Any other time, he would have been one of those friendly helpful country folks that Ethan liked so much. This time, though, when she was at her most vulnerable, the Universe sent her a Catch.

She made her way back to the bedroom, to the gun cabinet. Retro had stayed behind, frozen in front of the door, baring his teeth like he could rip through the wood with his will alone.

The gun cabinet - a safe, really - was locked tight. She remembered Ethan saying that the gun cabinet would be better in the bedroom for another reason, too. He'd won the argument handily by explaining that if someone broke in during the night, he wanted those guns as close to him as possible. "It just makes sense," he explained patiently, in that way of his. "Do you want them to find the guns on the way to our room?"

She reluctantly agreed, but she still hated it. Now, she was kind of glad it was back here, away from the drama taking place at the front of the house. Burns was still on the attack, and Abel was apparently still holding his own. She felt the urge to hurry, though. Burns wasn't going to be able to fight Abel off indefinitely. He may even need her help right now.

She got to the bedroom door and stopped. The key. Ethan kept it on the nightstand on his side of the bed - toward the window, another safety measure. She hurried around the foot of the bed and reached for the lamp, then stopped herself. The last thing she needed was to give Abel such a clear target. Instead, she felt underneath, patting with her palm all around the surface. It should be right here.

She checked again. The key was gone. She dropped to her knees, just in case it had been knocked to the floor, but running her hands over the carpet turned up no cold metal, rubber duck keychain. She could see it in her mind's eye. Right here. Since they had moved in, it had always been right here...

She stood up again and opened the drawer. It must have fallen in with Ethan's socks. The drawer was a mess - he thought folding socks was the biggest waste of time ever, and he just stuffed them into balls - so she started grabbing the balls and tossing them onto the bed to her right. As she emptied the drawer, she felt along the corners and way in the back, although how the key would have gotten there she didn't know.

When the drawer was empty and she still hadn't found it, she straightened up. Where else...?

Under the bed! Maybe Ethan knocked it off the table and didn't notice. Maybe he kicked it under the bed...She dropped to her knees again and reached as far as she could, her biceps pressing against the cold metal frame. Patting, patting...she almost screamed when her fingers touched rubber.

She caught the flat rubber duck-shaped ring and pulled it out, but already her heart was sinking. It was too light. She felt where the little chain attached, felt the ring, and then she felt it was empty.

That wasn't possible. The key was always here. Ethan had showed it to her every day for a week when they first moved in - "It's right here, Quinn. Don't forget." She had come to the side of the bed and touched it, every time, to make him happy. She was glad he wanted to protect her, glad he wanted her to know.

He had promised to teach her more about the guns this coming spring, and she'd been glad about that, too. It was his way of caring. He'd wanted to start earlier, before hunting season, but it was too cold out -.

Hunting season. Just rabbits and squirrels this time of year, and Ethan wasn't much of a hunter, but he would have taken a gun into the woods with him. He always took a gun. She imagined him getting ready in the mornings. Putting on his coat and hat, walking through the hall to the bedroom in his sock feet, and getting a weapon from the gun safe. Sometimes it was a shotgun, sometimes a rifle. Once in a while he took a pistol, too, checking if it was loaded and sliding the holster along his belt.

How many times had she seen him absent-mindedly stick that small copper key into his pocket, realize what he'd done, laugh at himself and then put it back on the side table? How many times had she seen him do it? Ten? Twenty? Fifty?

She sank onto the bed and sucked in a ragged breath. Tears burned her eyes and she swiped at them. Her throat closed against air and she clutched at the blanket under her on the edge of the bed - she didn't need a panic attack, not right now. *Breathe, Quinn. Breathe and think.*

But the sudden terror fought back, clawing through her chest, pushing small whimpers past her lips. She felt unable to move, unable to even stand, much less try to make rational thought happen. Her mind swirled with images of Burns, dead, Ethan dead, her dead in a few minutes. Retro would be alone if Abel didn't kill him. He would starve, or get lost in the woods. Maybe he could find his way to the neighbors by the -.

The neighbors. What had Abel called them? Rick and Patty? Her mind latched onto the names and brought them into sharp focus. Her eyes went to the window. Rick and Patty. They were help, less than a mile away. Within reach, if she could just be strong. If she could catch her breath and get herself together, if she could...

The sound of a gunshot pulled her off the bed to her knees on the floor. Her arms flew over her head and her throat let loose a strangled scream. Burns. She snorted a sob. "No, no, no..." she whispered, squeezing her eyes shut, like she could stop the truth.

She listened as carefully as she could, but no sound other than her own fearful heartbeat reached her ears. That bastard had killed Burns. Anger fought with fear in her gut, and for a moment she fought back a throat-full of vomit.

Pounding on the door made her cover her head again. Abel said something, his voice deep but too muffled. Retro broke into a barking fit. She heard his claws ticking toward her, down the hall, but then he stopped and turned again, still barking. Her instinct was to call to him, to snuggle his head and soothe his confusion and worry, but she couldn't risk Abel pinpointing her here in the house. As hard as it was, she needed to be still. She squeezed her lips together and willed Retro to come to her. For the first time, really, since the beginning of this terrible day, it occurred to her that she might die.

Another gunshot sounded again, and she heard a new sound. It took her a moment to place it, but then she did - splintering wood.

Abel was shooting the locks on the door.

Chapter Eleven

A bel staggered against the door and tried the lock. The damned dog - he hadn't seen that coming - had ripped most of his coat off and sank those God-awful teeth into his thigh, his forearm, and his calf. Abel's muscles burned enough that he was pretty sure there was blood, but he didn't bother checking. Time enough for that later.

He fell back from the door and leaned against the porch banister to steady himself. In the process he kicked over a little birdhouse looking thing that sat on the edge of the porch. It was a tiny house that looked kind of like this one, except on the side in fancy letters and red ink it said, *Ethan and Quinn Galloway*. He grunted at it, thinking *nice-ta-meecha, Quinn*. Then he lifted the rifle and took aim.

Woman wouldn't get away from him. She'd lied about her husband, hadn't she? She'd busted him in the head with a damned crowbar, of all things. He should have seen it coming, and he hadn't. It made him feel stupid, and Abel hated feeling stupid.

From the ruckus inside, he knew he'd have to shoot a second dog before he could get to Quinn. It was a shame. He liked dogs, and the German shepherd laying at the foot of the stairs was a beautiful specimen. Reminded him of a pup his best friend had a long time ago, when he was just a kid. That had been a good dog, and he'd wanted to own one just like it since he could remember. Maybe one day, but not today. He would kill the dog as soon as he got the door open. He was ignoring his wounds for now, but he also knew that he wouldn't be able to handle much more damage.

The woman would be worth it. She would have access to the money, the cars...everything he needed. Once he had that, he'd be all set. Of course, he wouldn't be able to keep her around like he'd thought. He could see that now. She was too much trouble.

The rifle kicked, but nothing he couldn't handle. Wood flew from a spot about two inches left of the door knob. He cursed, spread his stance a little, and aimed again. This time the knob twisted. He let out a satisfied grunt, aimed, and shot again.

The door knob stayed put, but he heard a small clink as the inner part of it fell to the hardwood floor inside. That brought a smile to his face. Then he heard Quinn whistle. His smile widened. The dog stopped barking.

His first instinct was to knock out the rest of the knob, put his eye to the hole and look inside. But Abel wasn't stupid and he knew that she might have a gun pointed at that eye hole. It wasn't likely, she wouldn't be thinking that clearly, but it was possible.

He shifted against the banister again. The burning in his calf was getting worse. He would need to do something about it soon, but right now he was too close.

It was funny how rich people moved to the back country, thinking they were some kind of farmer, when they were really just sitting ducks for guys like him. He wasn't special or fancy or even moral, and he knew it. It was the only way for guys like him to get ahead, wasn't it? He didn't have the good TV parents or the private schools or the car at graduation. The system had kept families like his poor and dumb, and whose fault was that?

The same rich people who were moving in here and buying up land, playing farmer, like they knew anything about living in the real world. They were the ones who never gave him a chance, and they were the ones who taught him that if he wanted anything, he might as well just take it.

Nobody was handing out the good life, were they? Like his daddy always said, "Fight for what you want, and never run from a fight."

So he ignored his pain, stood up tall against the porch post, and fired again. The door blew open like he'd kicked it.

Abel grinned and lowered the gun. Then he stuck his head inside, carefully, just in case the dog jumped at him. He didn't see anything, but his body was getting stiff, thanks to his wounds. No matter. He'd be finished here soon, and he could rest in that fine recliner he spotted in there. It better be worth the trouble. "Quinn Galloway!"

As soon as he yelled, he saw a flash of light from the corner of his eye. Turning, he picked out a set of headlights coming around a bend in the road. That would be Patty, coming home from work. It was too cold for anyone to be out running around for the fun of it, especially on roads as treacherous as these.

He knelt down until he was below the banister level and waited for her car to pass. It disappeared into the tree again, headed down the mountain and he turned his attention back to the house.

Chapter Twelve

Her first instinct was to roll under the bed, but then she immediately realized how stupid that was. The house wasn't large, and he would be able to find her in a matter of minutes if she tried that.

She had to get out. And she had to do it before he got to her.

Another gunshot pierced the air.

She jumped of course - it sounded like he was aiming a cannon down the hall. She pushed up from the floor and, before she could talk herself out of it, whistled.

The ticking of Retro's claws told her he'd heard. Thank God.

His head poked in through the bedroom door. He barked once, and she shushed him. What was the command for him to be silent? Ethan had told her, but her mind was too scattered to remember. "Retro," she whispered. He came to her.

Another shot startled them both, but this time she thought fast enough, when Retro turned away, to grab his collar. She was going to need him with her.

"Quinn Galloway." Abel's voice was sharp, angry.

The air whooshed out of her lungs. She gripped Retro's collar that much harder.

Her coat was in the living room. No way she was going after it. She glanced toward the closet, but did she really have time to worry about layers, or finding one of Ethan's old coats that had been shoved to the back?

No, she didn't. In fact, her feet had made the decision for her - she was already moving through the doorway, into the hall. It was less than a mile to the neighbors' house. She was wearing a sweater with a t-shirt under it. She could survive that. She had to - there was no time left. At least she was still wearing her boots.

She thought she heard a faint hum, but didn't take time to figure out what it was - probably the refrigerator running, and she wasn't about to die because of a refrigerator.

Abel had gained entrance, and she was without a weapon. She reached the door, found the knob. and slipped outside, dragging Retro with her. Hopefully Abel was busy out front and wouldn't know she was gone. He'd have to hunt. That would buy her time.

There was another problem, and now that she was out here, standing on the porch, she immediately realized the flaw in her thinking. It might be only a mile to the neighbors, but that was by road, and she couldn't get to the road, not without going around to the front of the house. Not without Abel seeing her.

That left the woods. The way she needed to go was steep and dangerous, full of briars and sharp drops where the rocks had given way long before America was a country. The biggest hurdle was a steep ravine, at least eighty feet deep, with a small creek at the bottom. The whole mess was scattered with loose stones, wet leaves under the deep snow, and about ten small crevices in the rock - not quite caves, but deep enough to hide any number of possibly dangerous animals. Getting to the bottom without breaking her ankles would be a feat, all by itself. Then she would have to climb the other side, make her way to the river and travel the bank to the neighbor's house.

She and Ethan had talked about clearing off this part of the land, thinking that water running out of the mountains would form a beautiful waterfall there. They even considered renting some equipment and making a nice walking trail to the bottom.

So many plans, and they were just getting started. Now it was over already, and it had all been for nothing. All the planning, the dreaming, the tossing around ideas and double and triple checking their finances. Ethan had given up a new truck last year, so they would have that much extra in the bank. Now Quinn wished that he'd bought that truck. She wished they still lived in Atlanta, where Ethan was secretly miserable but still alive.

Still gripping Retro's collar, just in case he decided to go back, she crouched and ran for the woods behind the dog pen. The air was frigid and immediately hurt her chest, but she ignored it and crunched through the knee high snow until she could slip behind a tree. At least it had stopped snowing for now. She desperately wished that the clouds would clear a little and offer her a few slivers of moonlight, because her flashlight was still in her coat pocket in the house.

She paused behind the tree, pulling Retro around in front of her so that he was hidden, too. As long as he didn't bark, they should be concealed well enough for the moment. She'd only run about fifty feet from the house to the trees cover, but her legs were already shaking with the effort of kicking snow out of her path and slogging through the wet. Her pants were soaked to the knees, about six inches above the boots she thought would be fine when she bought them.

This was not going to be a pleasant trip.

The sky stayed dark, but her eyes began to adjust a little. Still, she could only see about ten feet in front of her, and most of that was impassable. She noted a couple of fallen logs in her path and looked for a way around them. If she fell here, she would basically roll to the bottom of the ravine - that is, if she didn't slam her head against a tree and die first. The thought made her shudder and she pushed off, before she lost her nerve.

One lucky thing she noticed was the natural trails - small, clear areas, almost holes in the brambles, where deer and other critters made their way to the river from here. She could see two for sure, and maybe a third. All of them were small and hard to see, but she thought that if she looked closely and tried to be very careful, she could follow these trails to her destination.

One night not long after they'd moved in, she was coming from the chicken house when Ethan met her halfway across the yard for a kiss. She had snuggled in close and given him what he was after, but then they heard something froze them both. A scream. It wasn't exactly human, but it wasn't animal, either. They had stared at each other wide eyed, and she remembered the hair all over her body standing on end as the wavering high-pitched noise penetrated her ears.

"What is that?" she managed to get out, before Ethan shook his head and shushed her.

In the end, he didn't know either, and it took an hour of YouTube videos to figure it out. A mountain lion.

Retro looked around the woods and then whined up at her. He licked her hand, and she didn't know if he was worried, or just trying to reassure her. She didn't know - she was just thankful beyond belief to have him here. If she had to travel these woods alone...well, she wasn't sure she'd have the guts, to be honest.

She listened for a moment, and when she didn't hear anything but the rustle of Retro's fur against her and her own breathing, she pushed off the tree and headed away from the house.

The land began to slope downward almost immediately, making her feel a little bit like she was going to tumble head first into the ravine. Keeping one hand on various trees as she passed and the other firmly around Retro's collar in case he ran, she was walking blind and relying on the dog to let her know if she needed to stop or go around something. He wasn't trained for this, of course, but she knew that he wouldn't walk blindly off a cliff, either. If he stopped, she would, too. It was as simple and as dangerous as that.

Her boots crunched loudly in the snow, and if Abel was anywhere close she would be in real trouble. It wouldn't take much to pinpoint her out here, while she was too blind to see anyone if they were more than a few feet away. If he somehow got in front of her, she would slam right into him without Retro's input.

The thought almost paralyzed her, but she shook the thought out of her head and forced her feet forward.

The land was sloping farther now, enough that she had to slow down. In order to keep her balance, she reluctantly let go of Retro's collar. Thankfully, he stayed close. If she listened closely she could hear him panting. When a sharp branch caught her cheek, she hissed but didn't stop moving.

The first time her foot slipped out from under her, she was on her ass before she even knew what happened. Her arm had caught a slim tree trunk instinctively, but she still slid on her butt for a second before she got stopped. At the same time, she gasped hard enough that the shot of cold air in her lungs made her head hurt immediately, like a sort of brain freeze without the ice cream.

When she was still again, she moaned softly out of pure fear. She didn't want to go farther. She didn't want to climb down into this ravine. She just wanted to be home, warm and safe with her husband, and that wish was lost to her forever. No more silly jokes. No more walking by his side through the woods.

No more Ethan. He was gone, along with Burns and any plans to go happily through their twilight years. She sat very still and started to cry. Her tears were hot on her cheeks.

She knew she needed to move, but she just couldn't. The weight of her loss and fear was breathtaking now that she had a moment to consider it. For a moment, she wondered why she was even trying. Wouldn't it be better to just rest? To stay right here and just...pray? Sleep?

Follow Ethan? Be where he'd gone?

It sounded enticing. She had never considered it before, but it was one solution. Burns was probably dead, like Ethan, and that would be her fault, too.

Coyotes began to howl in the distance. Their reedy songs filtered through the trees and found her where she sat, perched on the ravine wall. Beside her, Retro shifted nervously and pressed in close. A low growl rumbled up from his chest.

He thought she was worth saving. Worth protecting.

Both dogs did. She remembered last December when both dogs had risked themselves for her. It had been the first good snow, not long after they moved in, and she was still enchanted with the idea of living in such a wonderland of nature. Every branch was covered, and snow sparkled as far as her eyes could see. While she had loved her life in Atlanta with Ethan, she missed the snow. Growing up in Nebraska she had hated it, but time and distance had softened her memories, and on that day she felt a visceral need to walk in it, to kick it and breathe it in and watch her own breath float away on the breeze.

So she had gone for a walk. She had watched her steaming breath and kicked the snow and felt the crisp, cold air against her skin. That day she decided that she and Ethan had made the right decision when they chose this place. She had been laugh-out-loud happy, until the moment the man stepped out of the woods.

He was standing just inside the tree line, and if he hadn't moved she would never have known he was there. That thought haunted her later - the fact that she could have waltzed right by, within three feet of him, and never have known.

But he had moved, and then several things happened at once. She had screeched and stumbled back, catching only a glimpse of his stubbled face with hard dark eyes and his black clothes. The barrel of his rifle stood out in sharp relief against the background of white snow. Before she could land on her butt, both Burns and Retro lunged forward, knocking the man's legs from under him and dropping him to the ground. Retro's paws were on the man's chest when she realized what was happening and squeaked their names.

They had come to her immediately. She had helped the man up and apologized through his cursing. When he stopped, she invited him in to meet Ethan and warm up with a cup of coffee, and that's how they'd first met Pop.

But it had always impressed her, the way Burns and Retro both had willingly ran toward the man with the rifle, all for her and without a thought for their own safety. Part of it was training, yes, but she had given no commands that day. They simply knew to protect her, and that's what they did. Even Pop, after he was warm and dry again, had commended them as good dogs and offered them a venison jerky treat.

That day, Ethan had finally been satisfied that she would be safe if he left her there alone for some reason. And he'd been right, until today.

She wondered if he felt better about his suicidal decision, knowing that the dogs were here for her. Or Pop, even, who had asked her multiple times to call him if she needed anything. Maybe Ethan had, for whatever reason, had thought she would be OK.

All of this danced around the real question - why? Why had he taken his own life like this? What could have happened to jar him so badly? Quinn and Ethan were practically inseparable - there was no room for secrets between them.

More importantly at the moment was another why - why was Abel Welch after her? If he was simply a drunk, he would have given up and gone home. If he wanted to rob her, he would have done it by now, or stolen into the house while she was out in the barn. There was no need to chase her outside if what he wanted was free for the taking. She had been busy in the barn, so she would never have known he'd gone inside. So why was he after her, in particular? As far as she could tell, she had never met him before today.

Retro whined and licked her hand, but kept his ears perked toward the coyotes and their mournful howls. She could feel the tension in his body. Then he put his big soft head against her cheek. *Get up. We have to move. We have to go.* She reached out one stiffening arm and hugged him. "OK, buddy. OK, we're going."

That was somewhat easier said than done. She'd been sitting still long enough that the cold and wet had seeped into her clothes, just as exhaustion had seeped into her muscles and despair had seeped into her mind. When she finally struggled up from the ground, using both hands on Retro's neck for balance, she thought that every bone in her body might snap.

She wanted to go home, but home would get her killed right now. So would sitting here in the woods. Winter was coming to an end, which meant food was scarce for the predators out here. She was food, and every one of those coyotes knew it. They might avoid her under normal circumstances, but they were in survival mode.

It was another hundred yards to the bottom of the slope, and then she had to cut to her left and traverse another slope to the bank of the river. After that, she needed to fight her way downstream to the neighbor's place, where she could find help.

What if they weren't home? Well, she doubted that was the case - who would have three kids out in weather like this in the middle of the night? The neighbors seemed a little wild, but she had no reason to think that they were bad parents. Also, tomorrow was a school day. Someone would be home.

She turned to fully face the ravine and the slope beyond. Wind funneled up from the river and smacked her in the face.

She sucked in a breath of freezing air that hurt her chest, and her teeth started to chatter. Her layered clothes weren't doing much to protect her.

Retro's ears perked up. He glanced over his shoulder, back the way they had come.

Was Abel coming? Had he figured out quickly that she was gone? Had he figured out that she came this way? It wouldn't be hard - her tracks were stark in the back yard's snow covering. In spite of how she felt, she wasn't actually all that far from the house. She needed to put some distance between him and herself.

So she tucked away her heartbreak and confusion and set to work doing just that. She pushed everything else out of her mind, and started slowly making her way toward the bottom.

Chapter Thirteen

It took Abel Welch twenty full minutes to conclude that Quinn Galloway wasn't home.

It made no sense - where the hell had she gone?

He sat in the recliner and sighed at how nice and comfortable it was, he found the phone and yanked it out of its base, and he discovered the boxes of photos on the dining room table. He picked those up and carried them back to the living room. On the way, he kicked something metal that made a soft *tink* against his boot. Kneeling down, he felt around on the hardwood until has hand closed around the item - a flashlight. He picked it up and stuck it in his pocket.

Then he went to the recliner and turned on the lamp, except that it didn't come on. He frowned at it, then just shrugged and got out the flashlight, figuring the bulb was blown. After looking through the photos - they were damned boring, if you asked him - he tossed them all into the fireplace. The small blaze that ate them turned green and blue and red for a moment. Pretty. Prettier than the pictures, anyway.

Well, except for one. It was a picture of Quinn on a beach somewhere. She was a lot younger, but she still just looked like a younger version of the lady who had nailed him with the crowbar. Same light freckles, same long blondish hair, same compact figure. No kids - he could tell. She didn't have that softness around her middle that mothers did. He decided to keep that one.

He held the picture in one hand and the flashlight in the other while he checked the fridge for anything good. Nothing decent to drink - who had no kids but still kept milk? - no sandwich fixings, either. He opened a plastic bowl and saw that it was roast beef. It looked good, but he didn't have time to eat it right now. Maybe later, after he'd corralled Quinn and brought her back here.

Then, picture still clutched in his hand, he stood in the center of the big room and looked around. There was the kitchen on one end, the living room on the other. The kitchen would be bright during the day, with enough windows to let in sun and, more importantly, to get a pretty clear view of the surrounding property. He didn't think anybody could sneak up on the house without their presence being noticed in a hurry.

The living room had lots of windows, too. One was right by the recliner. A man could see all the comings and goings from here, easy. Every car, every four-wheeler. Ethan Galloway must have been a nosy cuss. He knew it had to be Ethan's chair, because it was too deep for Quinn's short legs. Her feet wouldn't even touch the ground when she sat in it. He moved on to the bedroom.

He flicked the light switch, but nothing happened. He frowned and flicked it a few more times before he gave up. The snow must have knocked out a power line somewhere. Now that he thought about it, the fridge light hadn't come on, either. No matter - he wasn't looking for anything in particular, except for Quinn.

The big bedroom had a king-sized bed in it, a couple of dressers, and a long curved mirror on some kind of wooden stand. His momma had one of those once, a gift from her own momma before the TB killed her. If he remembered right, it had gotten broken in the fire that took their house and two of his little sisters when he was ten. He turned the flashlight away, mad that he'd thought about it right now.

The bed was made, and in here the curtains were drawn over the windows. Over in the corner, in a space that seemed too small for it, sat a black metal box with gold lettering on it. It was taller than him and twice as wide. He grinned, knowing exactly what that was - the gun safe. Everybody who could afford it had one in these parts, and he'd seen plenty just like this one. He wondered where the key was, then figured he would make Quinn tell him later.

His eyes dropped a little, toward the dark strip of floor that marked the space under the bed. She was little, she could be hiding under there.

He dropped to his knees and shone the light underneath. The action made him dizzy, and he realized that he was jonesing for another drink. Well, it would have to wait - the Galloways were evidently teetotalers, and he needed to find Quinn before he went back to Rick and Patty's on a beer run.

Well, it was just Patty's now, wasn't it?

His brain was starting to feel muddy, though, and he wondered if he should take the time to eat that stew after all. Maybe it would steady him.

He turned away from the bedroom doorway and stopped. Shined the light. Grinned. Because the answer to Quinn's whereabouts was right here in front of him.

The back door had a little window in it, the kind that wasn't big enough for anything but a quick look-see if somebody knocked. Quinn had hung a small blue curtain over it, one of those slinky kind that you could sort of see through. He wouldn't even have noticed, except that the curtain wasn't hanging right. It was caught in the door, like somebody had slammed it closed before the curtain could swing back out of the way. And he figured that's exactly what had happened. She'd slipped away, sometime before he came inside.

He opened the back door and stuck the flashlight out through the crack - just in case she was waiting there with that damned crowbar. When nothing moved, he stepped out and looked a little closer.

When he saw Quinn's footprints, headed for the dog pens, he chuckled and closed the door again. She was either out there in those pens, waiting for him to leave, or she was gone into the woods. In that direction, he knew for a fact that she had miles of hard traveling. It would get her to town, but not before she froze to death or got eaten by coyotes. Either way, he wasn't too worried.

When he came back to the living room, his eyes went to that recliner again. For a second he imagined Quinn and Ethan sat in the big chair together, her on his lap while they...did what? What did rich people do? Talk about their money? Make vacation plans? He didn't know, and he didn't much care. He took the picture in his mind and replaced Ethan with himself. Quinn would sit in his lap now, and they would definitely get a TV set. One of those giant ones that hung on the wall over the fireplace. Yeah.

This was the life he was supposed to have. This house, this wife, this chair. That truck in the driveway. Life had stolen it all over the years, but now...

Well, now was Abel's chance to get it back. It was his, after all, or it should have been. Everything came full circle, didn't it?

Chapter Fourteen

By the time Quinn was halfway to the bottom of the ravine, all she could hear was her own stumbling footsteps crashing through the forest and her own heartbeat thrumming in her ears. Her throat was raw with cold, her hands were numb and her feet were getting there quick, and her eyes blurred with tears every few steps, so that she had to stop and wipe at them.

Even without the benefit of a thermometer, she had no trouble figuring out that the temperature had dropped substantially. She was trying to remember what the radio weather guy had said this morning when she stumbled a little too fast down a particularly steep slope and tripped over a fallen log that lay hidden under the snow.

A short, sharp scream tore out of her throat before she clamped her lips shut. Her hands reached out instinctively, but not fast enough. She landed on her side, popping her temple against something hard under the snow. A rock? Another log? She didn't know, and she didn't care.

Retro came to her and snuffled her ear. She swatted him away and pushed up to a sitting position, worried that Abel was closer than she thought, that he'd heard the scream and was stomping in her direction even now. It took forced even breathing and counting to ten backwards and forwards before she remembered that none of those fears could be true. She would be able to see Abel or at least hear him, if he was moving in the woods behind her. If she couldn't make him out, the odds were good that her scream was swallowed by the pillowy snow and would never reach his ears.

"OK," she whispered, panting. "OK, Retro. Good doggo. Good boy."

Retro's tail waved a little, but his attention wasn't on her anymore. He was looking out across the ravine to the opposite upslope. She froze where she sat, wondering what he sensed but not seeing anything.

Of course, the moon was still missing from its place in the sky, so there wasn't much to see beyond a dull gray-scale landscape, only broken by black tree trunks against the featureless ground.

Sitting here, she knew, was going to get her killed. Either Abel would catch up - she didn't believe for a minute that he wouldn't follow those footprints - or she would succumb to the cold. As far as the coyotes...well, she kept an eye open for trees to climb, just in case. Right now, they were almost welcome, compared to facing off with the drunken bastard behind her. She was just standing up, using a skinny frozen tree for support, when she paused, thinking she heard something.

Abel stiffened beside her.

She listened closer, holding her breath and letting her mouth fall open a little.

There it was - a faint hum, riding the wind. She thought it might just be a plane overhead, except that Retro was paying too much attention. He didn't care about planes, so this was something else.

But what? An ATV? It could be. She pictured Ethan's, a red and green monster, crouched in the barn. She pictured the key, hanging just inside the barn door on a rusty nail that had probably been there since Carter was president. She had said that to Ethan once, and ever since they had called it the Carter nail. She wondered if Abel had somehow found it, and if he was coming after her right now.

That was impossible. Their ATV was four-wheel drive, but there was no way it could make it through these trees. Just the fallen timber would wreck the thing before Abel got twenty feet from the tree line.

But what if he thought she was on the road? He might - she could have cut through the yard and then made a sharp right. That would have put her in the clear at least.

Now that she thought about it, she wondered why she hadn't done that. Why instinct had driven her into the woods, instead of down the road. She might have been at the neighbors' house by now if she had done that.

Of course, if Abel was riding around on Ethan's ATV, she might be dead by now, too. Something had put her here instead of there, and she decided to trust it, whatever it was. The woods were harder to navigate, but she would just keep going. Better exhausted than caught in a madman's headlights on an old dirt road, unarmed and out of options.

But this didn't sound much like an ATV, either, and the more she listened, the more she thought it might just be...a car? Who would have a car out at this time of night in these conditions? It was suicide, especially on these roads.

A flash of brightness lit up the treetops just to her left, making her gasp. It was a car. Those were headlights. Someone was on the road. She started running that way, wanting to yell, knowing that no one in a car would be able to hear her.

So she ran. The engine revved louder - it was climbing the mountain, headed toward her house. She hoped it was the man named Rick, looking for his buddy Abel. Or maybe Rick and Patty had gotten into a fight, and now he was leaving.

And then, after the sound filled the forest around her, it began to fade. There were no more flashes of light, no more revving engines. It was gone almost as quickly as it had come. She stood very still, listening, to make sure it hadn't stopped at her house. Then she turned away and kept going. Her frantic run had sapped much needed strength and lengthened the distance to the river.

By the time she made it the bottom of the ravine, she was nearly too weak to stand. The cold seemed to be stealing the energy from her bones and leaving only dead stumps behind. She wasn't positive how she was still moving, unless she was running on pure adrenaline.

How long would that last? Till she got to Rick and Patty's house? Or would she fall somewhere beside the river and be unable to get up again? Maybe they would find her in the spring.

God, she hoped the kids wouldn't find her. That would be gruesome, and the experience would probably scar them for life. Especially if some animal found her first. The thought made her stomach lurch with nausea, and she blinked the idea away.

And what about Ethan? If she died out here what would become of his poor remains? She didn't want to think about that. She didn't want to think about his dad, either, who would have to spend maybe his last bit of time on earth burying the last of his loved ones. That thought almost brought her to her knees. Earnest was nothing but a wonderful man, a good dad, and a loving and loyal husband even though his wife had been gone for a while now. Quinn had never seen him down so low that he didn't have a smile and a hug for her. The thought of breaking his heart even once nearly broke hers.

But it also brought her to her senses. She pushed off the tree trunk and started walking again, following the little frozen creek that cut through the bottom of the ravine. Retro turned his attention back to her and trotted along, keeping his eyes on the hill ahead of them. She didn't know what he saw or heard, but it definitely had him concerned. She even heard a growl rumble up from his throat now and again, soft but menacing. Whatever it turned out to be, he was ready for it.

By the time she got to the river, she was practically crawling. Every part of her body was either numb or aching, including her head. It felt like one more step and her eyes would pop right out of their sockets, they hurt so badly. She wondered if this was what freezing to death felt like. She hadn't thought it would hurt so much. She thought she read that it was like being warm and slowly losing focus, until the person simply laid down for an eternal nap. It wasn't supposed to hurt.

But it did, and the hurt kept her going. She was surprised to find this reserve of strength inside herself, bubbling up every time she thought about sitting down to rest. It kept her heart beating steady and her eyes on the trail ahead. It also seemed to be keeping an inventory of her aches and pains, but maybe that was her fuel right now. If she felt anything at all, there was still a chance, right? That became her mantra - *there's still a chance, there's still a chance* - right up until the moment she spotted lights through the trees. Rick and Patty were just ahead, and she almost cried with relief.

The riverbank was covered with snow, but underneath she could feel her feet sliding in mud that sucked at her heels. She was taking her time, feeling for every next step, being careful to keep from sliding into the icy water. She couldn't see it, but the roar of the water meant that it was moving fast. If she went in, she might not get back out.

But now, with the end in sight, she sped up. Deadfall cracked under her steps and she had to grab a branch here and there to keep her feet under her, but she was practically running by the time she broke through into the small clearing.

Three big floodlights flashed on, illuminating both Quinn and the rest of the clearing, which covered about an acre and fronted the riverbank. No one would call the area a lawn, exactly, but there were brightly colored toys poking up through the snow here and there, two or three old trucks parked nearby, and she thought she saw a swing bench over near the water, where two people could sit and talk and watch the wide river pass. A wall of trees rose up beyond the clearing, lending almost perfect privacy.

In front of the trailer was a black patch. It was apparently a parking spot, because there was an older sedan sitting there. Beside it, a blank, car-shaped spot told Quinn that there was a vehicle missing.

Rick and Patty's trailer was once blue, but the color had powdered and faded over too many years in the weather. Rust streaked the metal vertically, where rivets and bolts had begun to disintegrate. The tongue of the trailer, also rusted, poked out of one end. It looked like the young couple had tried to brighten it up - or camouflage it - with various plants, but there were only empty plastic pots there now, trailing a few dead leaves and vines. Above that, a wide skinny window shone dully, covered by what looked like a yellow curtain with a ruffle at the bottom.

Quinn noticed that a small porch jutted out from the back of the trailer, another spot to sit and watch the water. There was no matching porch on the other side, near the parking spots. Just a set of what looked like concrete steps leading up to a door. Since those steps had been cleared at some point today, she headed that way.

Pounding on the door hurt her hand, but she didn't stop. She wasn't sure she could stop, not until someone with a friendly face answered.

But no one did. She called out a painful hello, but only silence greeted her when she finally stopped to listen. There was only the softly falling snow and the wind moving through the trees up on the ridge, which sounded more mournful than the coyotes, if that was possible. No shuffling from inside. No voices, not even the muted tones of a television.

She stood on tiptoe and leaned as far to the right as she could, where a small window acted as a sort of sidelight. It was covered by another curtain, this one some washed out shade of green, but it was sheer. She was just able to get one eye close enough to peer inside.

Brown carpet, pizza boxes, and several cups and glasses littered the living room in front of a TV that was too large for the space. A few toy cars and trucks were piled together on one of the gray sofa cushions. A stack of children's books sat on the end table.

Beyond those things, the brown living room carpet ended at gray linoleum. The kitchen, which looked spotlessly clean from here. It stood out, compared to the rest of the room. White appliances gleamed under the fluorescents, and a single yellow cup sat beside a black coffee pot on the wood counter.

In fact, there was only one thing out of place in the entire room, but it was enough to draw a small gasp from Quinn. A bloodstain smeared the linoleum and two of the lower cabinet doors, dark red against all the white cleanliness. Above it, on the countertop, was a slim white phone, it's curled cord handing halfway down to the floor.

She lowered herself firmly back to the porch and stood there, trying to figure out what to do. First of all, where was everyone? Had the dad or mom done something to one of the kids? Had they done something to each other? That had definitely been blood.

Worse, what if Abel had hurt these people before he left? What if the whole family was dead, piled in the back yard? Or in the river, where they might never be found?

Her mind kept throwing out horror stories, and her body kept sinking, until she was crouched on the top step, pressed against the side of the trailer. She knew she needed to get a handle on herself, but she couldn't seem to do that. The more she thought about it, the more she was sure that Abel had caused this...whatever...that happened here. It just seemed too convenient that she'd caught him out moving around in this kind of weather, in his condition.

Why on earth would he have left the safety and shelter of his home, unless he didn't want to be caught there?

The leaps of logic were large and inexplicable, but Quinn didn't even care. In truth, she knew that all sorts of explanations might be the right one - maybe the blood was from a deer. Maybe this Rick guy had a tendency to hurt his wife or kids. Maybe Patty had the same tendencies and took them out on her husband. Maybe Abel had nothing to do with any of this.

But she'd seen that wildness in his eyes when he showed up at her barn door, and she was comfortable assuming that he had done something to the small family. In fact, she would have bet her life on it.

One thing was certain, she wasn't going around to the other porch.

Instead, she forced herself to stand up straight and knock again, just in case. When that didn't get any results, she took a deep breath and tried the door knob. It clicked a little, but then it turned and the door swung open.

Retro nosed in near her knees, but she told him to stay. She knew he would bark if someone came, and she needed him outside right now, on guard.

The smell hit her first. A tangy sort of odor that made her wrinkle her nose, even though she couldn't quite place it. Underneath that she caught a whiff of cooked meat, maybe hamburger. The smell turned her stomach.

A pile of muddy shoes sat beside the door on a rug. All sizes, from men's work boots to the small pairs of sneakers that obviously belonged to a little girl. On the wall above, several jackets and coats hung from hooks. A few framed pictures, mostly of the kids, hung on the walls of the living room. She made her way inside, closed the door very quietly behind her, and called out, "Hello? Anybody home?"

There was no answer, except for the creaking of the trailer as the wind gusted around it. Still, she did the same thing twice more, just in case. She didn't want to end up getting shot for trespassing, or scare somebody to death if they were just asleep.

When she finally decided to move, she wasn't sure whether to go check the bedrooms or go straight to the phone on the kitchen counter. She stared at the closed door off the far side of the living room for a while, trying to decide. Then, with a last regretful look at the doors, she headed over to the phone.

Chapter Fifteen

Dupree Captin, known to pretty much everyone around as just Cap, finished splitting the last of the wood and buried the head of his maul in the remaining stump. No need to put it away - he'd be using it again first thing in the morning. Then he crossed his arms, reared back, and checked the cloud cover. Snow coming in the next fifteen minutes or so. He grunted to himself and headed for the house.

He didn't need the wood, his gas furnace ran just fine, but he had discovered that splitting wood got the kinks out. Men his age had a tendency to cuddle up with Judge Judy and The Guiding Light, but Cap didn't much like sitting around watching TV. He had better things to do. Besides, if he sat around too long his joints would get stiff. This weather didn't help, either. This way, he stayed limber and he also made a little spending money on the side.

He didn't spend much of it, to be honest. No, his pension was plenty for their needs. He kept most of it in a jelly jar under the corner of his bed, waiting for the day that his nephew Brice snooped around long enough to find it. That'd be a fun day.

He walked through the snow to the back porch, then up the steps and into what his sister Mary called the mud room. He didn't call it that, he just called it the place he kept his boots and coveralls. It was actually the original back porch, until his dad, rest his soul, built it in for the washer and dryer. That was, oh, going on forty years ago now. Cap had liked it better as a porch.

But it kept Mary from fussing that he tracked in mud, and that made it all right.

Inside, he kicked off his brogans and swiped his toboggan from his head. It was an old, raveled thing, but it kept the cold out. Chill air swept across his bald head and gave him a shiver, but he ignored it, shrugged out of his coveralls, stripped them off his legs and hung 'em up in a nail to dry.

Through the kitchen door he could see Mary at the stove, stirring something that smelled warm and meaty. She was holding a dish towel in her free hand. Her red hair, streaked with plenty of silver these days, was pulled back into a short ponytail. "You makin' stew?" he asked, coming through the door and closing it behind him to keep out the cold.

She was dressed in jeans and a green t-shirt, with a different kind of green cardigan over that. She turned to him and smiled, shifting the wrinkles around her mouth a little. "I thought pork and sweet potato stew would be good. They're calling for eighteen inches," she answered, looking his up and down to make sure he wasn't dripping on her floors.

"You make bread today?" He came over and sniffed at the pot she was stirring. His belly growled.

She swished her dish towel at him. "Scoot. I'll do biscuits."

He studied a spot on the ceiling for a moment. "How long?"

She put the dish towel on the counter beside the stove and turned to him. Her gaze was serious, and a little worried. "Are you still thinking about the Galloways?"

"I am."

"Why don't you just call? I'm sure everything is fine."

"Tried that, got that busy tone you get when the line's down."

"Well, it happens. You aren't in any shape to do what you're thinking about doing." She pursed her lips and turned away, to the sink. Sudsy water sloshed a little when she started scrubbing a plate.

"And what do you think I'm thinking about doing?"

"Going over there." She tossed a look over her shoulder. "You know you are, and I know you are."

"What makes you think that?" He scratched his head and stared at her.

She answered without bothering to look at him. "Oh, come on, Cap. I know you better than I know myself."

He chuckled at that. "I doubt I can make it. Roads will be bad."

"You'll take the Gator."

He knew he would, but he was surprised she'd thought of it. Maybe she did know him better than he thought. He shoved his hands into his pants pockets and stayed quiet a minute, pretending to think it through. "That'd work."

"Why?" This time she turned around and grabbed the dish towel again. She wiped her hands. "Why worry about it? They're probably fine, and you're an eighty year old man."

"Seventy-seven."

"Whatever. You'll get out there and get yourself killed, and they'll be snug inside. They won't even know you're there." Mary leaned awkwardly against the stove, favoring her left leg. It was a gesture most people would miss, but not Cap. He'd seen it too many times. She was hurting again. He nodded at it. "You need to get that checked?"

"No. Just rest."

"What if they ain't, Mary? Snug inside, I mean?" He paused and tried to articulate the niggling worries that had been growing in the back of his mind all day like seeds pushing up out of the ground. "I know damned well what I heard this morning. I also know how Quinn sounded on the phone."

"The gunshots, right?"

"Gun *shot*. One. Yes. Also, Quinn sounded messed up, Mary. You should have heard her."

"So? She said Ethan was missing, right? She was just concerned."

Cap shook his head and walked on through to the living room instead of bothering to answer. Mary made logical sense, but he couldn't really explain this hunch that something bad was happening across the mountain. Hell, he couldn't explain it to himself, much less her.

Part of it was probably because of that dream he had last week, and he acknowledged that. In it, Ethan came to Cap's house, carrying a rifle. Mary gave them supper and asked where Quinn was. Ethan said he didn't know. Cap remembered that, plain as if it was real. "I don't know," Ethan said around a mouthful of biscuit, shaking his head. In the dream, that had scared Cap. He tried to ask more questions, tried to make Ethan tell him where Quinn might be, but he found he couldn't talk.

The whole thing made no sense, and Cap forgot all about it until this morning when Quinn called. By the time he hung up the phone, uneasiness was gnawing at the base of his skull. It had only ever happened one other time in his life, that feeling - knowing - that something bad was happening. The last time, he'd watched his dad walk into a mine. He'd been about ten, he reckoned, and he walked with his dad to work every morning before he went on past to school. Every morning they walked together, and every morning Cap watched his father disappear into the earth before going on. On the morning he had this feeling, his dad never walked out again. There was an accident with some of the explosives, and by the time they righted the rail car, his dad was dead.

It was an awful feeling back then and he'd ignored it.

He didn't want to make that mistake again.

Mary called him a little later and they ate. He stayed quiet, not wanting to hear her harping at him. Maybe, if he was honest, he was trying to talk himself out of going, too. When he finally looked up from his empty bowl, she was shaking her head at him.

"Don't bother," he said, carrying his bowl from the table to the sink about ten feet away.

"I won't," she answered. "You old bat."

He laughed at that, then went to his gun safe in the hall to get some steel courage.

The Gator was like a dune buggy, but built rugged for challenging terrain. Big knobby tires, a steel frame with a roll bar, and highly engineered suspension made it ideal for traversing Cap's Abel mountainous surroundings. It had a windshield, too, but that wouldn't be enough to shield him from the cold by much. But it wasn't too far, and hopefully this was a wild goose chase anyway. Maybe he'd get there, find them as safe as Mary said, and feel like a damned fool.

That'd be just fine with him. He'd have a laugh and a cup of coffee and take his leave.

By the time he got dressed and hit the road, it was snowing harder and dark. On the one hand, he agreed with Mary that he was being a damned fool, but on the other he didn't want to be the damned fool that let a friend down. And he considered Ethan and Quinn Galloway his friends. Not too many folks, even around here, thought to stay in touch with their older acquaintances, even ones that had been around as long as Cap had. The world moved on, and mostly he was fine with that, but it was nice to sit around a back yard fire with a few friends and a snort of brandy now and then. Ethan and Quinn provided those opportunities for old Cap, and even Mary, when she was feeling up to it. All by itself, that felt like a true thing to Cap.

He considered the younger couple his friends, and friends helped one another.

The road off his property was a half-mile of good driveway if he went out to the main road. It was a full mile of rutted mess if he went the back way. Normally the back way was faster, but tonight he wasn't so sure. If he hit deep snow and dug in the Gator, he was stuck. The main road would take longer, but he knew he'd make it. He decided on the main road.

Calling it a main road was being mighty generous anyway. It was a single paved lane, what they called chip and tar, rough on his tires and prone to breaking up under the temperature changes and the pressure of heavy traffic. It had been potholed to the point of dangerous before the first snow hit this winter, so he was going to have to be careful now. A bad pock or a fallen branch in the road could bend his frame if he hit it wrong. He wasn't too worried.

The road, once he got away from the house, was damned eerie in his headlights. More than once his tired old eyes saw fog that wasn't there when he blinked and looked again, like he was being followed by ghosts. It wisped between the trees and turned his head at nearly every turn, and by the time he got to the end of the driveway he was so on edge that his hands hurt from gripping the steering wheel too hard.

At the entrance to the public road he stopped and listened. He wasn't sure what he was listening for, exactly, but everything about this night was making his gut curl in apprehension.

Maybe Mary was right, he thought, not for the first time. She was a worry-wart, but that didn't mean there was nothing to worry about. He reached over to his side and touched the rifle that lay across the bench seat beside him. Then he looked both ways and pulled out. The trip around the mountain to the Galloway place would take him about fifteen minutes on a good day, but in these conditions it was more likely to cost at least an hour. Maybe more, if no one had forged tracks in the snow. He could see it taking him half the night.

He took an inventory of his toolbox. It was actually a big black Tuff Box, strapped to the back of the Gator. It contained the usual - a small ratchet and socket set, a lug wrench, a spare tire, the usual fluids - gas, oil, transmission fluid. A few other odds and ends had found their way in there over the years, too - a shovel, a tow rope, extra ammo for the rifle and a handgun he liked to carry. There was even a rain jacket folded up in the bottom of the box, just in case. Regular stuff, but he felt better having it with him.

Cap was the kind of man who liked to be prepared.

The snow blowing in his headlights was mesmerizing if he stared at it too long. He needed to keep his eyes moving and watch for...what? He was starting to feel a little ashamed of himself. What did he think he was going to find out here in the middle of the night?

But he still couldn't shake that creeping dread, so he drove on.

He didn't know, but that feeling was driving him hard, and he knew he'd be sick if he didn't follow up on it this time. If he was honest - and he was, generally - he knew he was trying to absolve some sin from the last time.

What sin, he didn't know. He'd been a child then, still in primary school. There was nothing he could have done besides begging his Pap to stay away from the mine that day. And he knew Pap would have rubbed his head, laughed, and reassured him. Then Pap would have walked into that mine anyway, same as he did every day of Cap's young life. It wouldn't have changed a thing.

He drove slowly, feeling the occasional lurch as his tires found a patch of ice here and there. Beyond his headlights, the night was as black as the inside of that mine he was just thinking about. He knew these roads, knew these woods. He knew that in general there was nothing to worry about, but he still couldn't shake the tension creeping up his neck and laying across his shoulders. It was there to stay, at least until he was finished with this unholy night.

He wondered if he shouldn't have at least called for back-up. There were a couple of neighbors within shouting distance, and he'd called on them once or twice to help with some farm chore or other over the years. Ollie Wake would have come, for sure. Probably Jersey too, if he wasn't busy birthing the calves that earned him his nickname.

Well, it was a little too late now.

Cap kept to the hilly side of the road, against the ditch, because the other side was a nearly sheer drop into a hollow below. It was at least fifty feet deep and he'd wind up at the bottom if a tree didn't stop him first. Problem was, they'd logged this area year before last, so any trees growing would be young and likely to snap under the weight of the Gator. If Cap didn't break his neck on the way down, he'd likely freeze to death in the creek at the bottom before somebody found him.

Well, that was a pleasant thought. It'd be tomorrow before Mary reported him missing, and, depending on the snow, it could be a week before somebody noticed the wreckage. "Being damned morbid tonight, Cap," he told himself, even though he couldn't hear his voice over the grinding roar of the machine.

Chapter Sixteen

Rick and Patty's phone was dead, too. Quinn had known it was a long shot, but that didn't stop her frustrated tears as she hung up and looked around again. She carefully avoided looking at the blood.

Who was she going to call, anyway? No one could get here, most likely. Not the police, not anyone she knew. Tonight, there was only her and Abel Welch. She'd never felt so alone in her life.

Of course, she'd never actually been alone in her life, either. She'd gone from a comfortable, if sad, home to a college career with roommates. From there, she had almost immediately married Ethan, and they had been together ever since. To say she'd been sheltered her whole life, well, that was an under-statement.

She needed to think, and this was as good a place as any to do it. For now, anyway. She had no idea where Abel was at the moment - was he headed down the road, following her here? Was he still at the house messing around? Had he passed out somewhere? The uncertainty gnawed at her because she had no idea what move to make.

If she knew he was gone, she would head back to the house. At least there she was familiar with her surroundings and had access to most anything she might need. Without him standing between her and Ethan, she could even get to the gun safe's key and defend herself properly.

But she wasn't there, and she wasn't sure she could go back. Meeting Abel on the road, in the dark, would be near suicide.

The word caused her belly to churn.

She looked around and spotted the refrigerator. Thirsty. She was so thirsty. She went over and opened it, prepared for anything. But when the light flashed on there was only normal refrigerator stuff - a gallon of milk, half gone, a few of those plastic containers for leftovers, two slices of pizza on a saucer. It was so normal that tears burned her eyes again. What she wouldn't give for normal right now.

On the bottom shelf were two brightly colored cardboard boxes, one blue and one red. She had to smile a little - there was obviously a decent Coke-versus-Pepsi battle going on in this house. The Coke box was emptier.

She reached in for one and popped the tab. She normally didn't drink any sort of cola, because the acid and carbonation irritated her stomach. But tonight, she needed the calories and she needed the cold liquid to soothe her aching throat. It tasted like heaven, and she drank half the can before she stopped to breathe.

She finished it, shuddered, and threw it into the half-full trash can in the corner of the kitchen.

Then she froze, because she realized that if something terrible had happened here, she had just given the police cause to think she had something to do with it.

The thought gave her a flash of fear, but then it was just gone again. As if her brain had reached its limit of things to worry about, and this one thing was so far down the list it could be discarded. She had to agree, because at this point she couldn't see that far ahead. Police? Clues?

Quinn was willing to settle for survival.

And what exactly did survival mean, on this night?

Her husband was dead, her home wasn't safe, and she was on her own in a snowstorm. There was a madman chasing her. She had very few ways to defend herself if Abel caught her, especially now that he was armed with the rifle she so stupidly left outside earlier.

She knew that if she survived this, she was going to have to face the fact that Ethan was really gone, but right now her mind just wouldn't let her do it.

Right now, the fact that she was in a stranger's house made her nervous. She didn't want to be here, and she couldn't go home. So what were her options? She couldn't just keep running around in the woods until spring.

What would Ethan do?

It was another running joke between them. He was a little over five years her senior, and he liked to play that card as a last resort when he was losing an argument. It never worked. But now she saw the value of such a question, regardless of how many times she had rolled her eyes when he said it. She didn't know what to do right now, and she would have given her own beating heart to have him here with her. That was impossible, of course, but maybe in her own way, she could figure it out.

What would Ethan do?

Well, first of all, he would be armed, so that was out. What else? He wouldn't run into the woods, that was for sure. She had gambled on finding some help, but that had been wrong.

Ethan would have stood his ground. He was an easy-going man who let a lot of life's little insults slide, but he also defended his boundaries. Could she do that? If so, how?

She could check this place for weapons. She couldn't stay here - it was too weird - so that meant going home. Trying to get across the mountain to Cap's house would just be a different kind of suicide, because she would just end up frozen to death in the woods somewhere.

But here, she had access to at least some helpful things. There was a coat hanging by the door, for starters. It looked big for her, but not so big that she couldn't use it. She thought about Patty and the few times she'd seen the woman driving by, and guessed that maybe they were close to the same size. She might have dry clothes that would fit Quinn.

That is, if Quinn was brave enough to open those bedroom doors and look. She eyed the closest one and shivered.

Then anger surged through her - she was being pathetic. Now she was afraid of doors? How stupid could one woman be?

Come to think of it, everything she'd done tonight felt pathetic. She had fallen apart when she realized what Ethan had done, she had run away from her home and the drunk. She had defended herself with a crowbar, which was pretty cool, but that was a small blip in the general idiocy she had shown so far tonight.

In the years after her baby brother died, Quinn and her father had watched Quinn's mother slowly crumble into a woman they didn't know. She went from being a happy wife and good mother to living her life as an alcohol soaked shell that barely looked up from her television. It was terrifying as a child, and Quinn had so many times wished for her mother to toughen up, to remember that she still had a child who needed her. In the end, Quinn and her dad simply lived around her mother, taking up the slack and managing as best they could.

Her mother had never toughened up. Her mother had died under the weight of her weakness and pain and fear.

All of Quinn's reactions tonight would be understandable under the circumstances, but that was all they were - reactions. She was a grown woman. She could handle a drunken man, and she could take back her home. If she was lucky, he was the one passed out somewhere in the woods, freezing to death.

She wasn't lucky, not right now, but she wasn't a wilting flower, either. One way or another, she was going to have to face Abel Welch. She was going to have to go home and deal with Ethan's decisions. She was going to have to bury Burns, report to the authorities, and clean up the wreckage that was her life. It was going to be hard, but unless she wanted to follow Ethan into the afterlife tonight, she had to do it.

She heard movement outside on the porch and froze for a moment, then remembered that Retro was out there, waiting for her. He was a good dog, and she was glad that at least she had him for company tonight. But he was probably getting cold. She walked to the door, opened it, and let him inside to warm up.

He whined up at her, sniffed her hand, and then went to check out the rest of the room. He looked huge in the small space.

She finally worked up the nerve to open the closest closed door and flip on the light. It was a bedroom, like she'd guessed, but that was stretching the definition. A mattress lay flat on the floor, covered in a stained brown quilt. She didn't want to touch it, so she scooted sideways around the wall to the closet. Inside, she found pink - this had to be the little girl's room.

She left and went to the next room, picking up an extra hair band from a small dresser as she left.

The next room had to belong to the boys. It smelled like sweat and food, and a set of bunk beds lined one wall. She closed the door without going inside.

Where was Rick and Patty's room? Or Abel's, for that matter? She didn't want anything of his, but she wondered where he had been sleeping, at least. Maybe he lived on their sofa.

She turned in a slow circle and scanned the room, then realized that there was a hallway. It was separated from the rest of the room by a tall bookshelf that looked homemade. Walking around it - carefully, just in case - she discovered two more doors. No, wait. Three - two on one side of the hall and one across from them. All were closed. She opened the one that was alone on her right and found a bathroom with a pile of clothes on the floor and an inch of water in the tub, as if someone had left in the middle of running their bath water. There was even moisture on the mirror with the faint hint of a finger drawn smiley face. One of the kids had been bathing, maybe. She closed the door again.

She felt lucky that she hadn't run across anything horrific so far, but she was getting nervous again now. "Well," she said out loud, "Didn't I just say it was time to toughen up? What's behind door number four?"

Before she could think anymore, she reached out and twisted the knob. The door swung open, revealing a laundry room that smelled like stale cigarette smoke, strong enough to make her eyes water a little. There was another mattress in here, in the opposite corner as the ancient looking washer and dryer. Maybe Abel stayed in here.

There was a duffle bag at the foot of the mattress, and a pile of grungy looking clothes near the head, like he was using it for a pillow. She made a face and went to see what was in the bag.

On top she found a few balled up pair of socks that had been white about a decade ago. Under that she found a glass jar with clear liquid. Opening the lid, she sniffed and jerked her head back. Whoa - Abel liked his home brew strong. The last thing in the bag was a small picture album, the kind that was on one picture to a page. It was nearly in shreds, as if he looked through it every single day at least once. The first picture in the album was an old one - two boys in cut off pants and cowboy boots, both about ten years old. They were grinning hard at the camera and had an arm flung across each other's neck. Was this Abel as a child?

She wanted to look through the rest of the photos, but something told her not to worry about it right now. She felt the need to hurry up, to get out of this place and go home. The longer she spent here, the more likely the chance that she would end up facing Abel here in this unfamiliar place. She didn't want that. She wanted to be home.

She was going to face him. She'd never been the type to run, and her actions this evening, now that she had a moment to regroup, felt shameful. Ethan had made her life so comfortable that she was unused to dealing with things herself.

Not that she had ever in her life been in this situation. Maybe it was natural to run, but she felt like Ethan would be ashamed of her actions.

Of course, if Ethan was here, she wouldn't be in this situation, would she?

Shaking that thought out of her head, she stuffed the skinny album into the back pocket of her jeans. There would be time to check it out later. Right now, she had one more door to check, and time was ticking. She shut off the lights and closed the door to that room.

Then she stopped in the hall. Wait a minute - was the electricity back on? Had someone come and fixed it? Or had it always been on and Abel had sabotaged her electricity specifically? The thought made her cold all over again.

She walked quickly to the final door. This one was ajar, so she used a toe to push it the rest of the way open.

This room, compared to the rest of the house, was lovely. Done in cabbage roses and pale yellow, it was nearly spotless. Patty cared about this room.

The queen sized bed sat against one wall, the foot jutting out into the center of the room. Across from that, on the opposite wall, there was a door that led into a master bathroom. The bed was made - it even had one of those devilsome bedskirts - and turned down, like the couple was getting ready for bed at any moment. A pair of soft looking lavender slippers sat in the floor on one side of the bed and the whole room smelled nice. Some scent that reminded her of baby powder.

So where were they? Quinn hadn't found any bodies. She hadn't seen any sign of a struggle besides that one area in the kitchen. It had to be at least three in the morning right now. Where was everyone?

There were two dressers in the room, the low kind with wide mirrors on top. An assortment of pretty trinket boxes graced the surfaces of both of them. For jewelry, maybe? Quinn walked over and opened on, and saw a collection of small colorful rocks. She smiled, thinking that this was probably a child's treasure, kept safe by mom.

In this room, she went to the closet and opened the door. She'd left the kids closets alone, because she doubted there would be anything helpful inside, but mom and dad's room was a different story. Clothes, shoes, a few shelves in the back, but they only held random books and boxes. Mostly the closet was full of scrubs.

The bathroom didn't hold anything of value to her, either. A shower, a toilet, and a pile of makeup on the vanity.

She turned away and decided that she'd wasted enough time in this house. She needed to leave.

Retro had taken off, exploring the rest of the house, but now he found her in the master bedroom. He had something in his mouth. When she looked closer, she saw that it was a bloody strip of material, maybe flannel. Somebody's shirt?

She gave him the command to drop it and he obeyed. "Come on, boy, let's get out of here."

Chapter Seventeen

A bel heard the truck before he saw the lights. It was a barely discernible growl that rode the wind, and it was coming from the main road. Who the hell would be outside at a time like this? He'd spent the last little while sitting in the recliner, thinking and dozing and waiting for Quinn to come back. She had to come back eventually, and she had gone the one direction he knew she wouldn't find help. He'd seen Patty's car heading out, and he knew that nobody was home at their place. Still armed with the rifle, he stepped out onto the porch to see who'd come to visit.

The headlights were a white glare across the freezing landscape, cutting sharply toward the tree line across from the house. He leaned against the partially destroyed front door frame and watched them bounce closer and closer. Then he glanced down at the foot of the steps that led to the front porch. Ethan's body was almost completely covered with snow now. Any other time, Abel would think the scene was almost festive, with the cedar branches hanging low with clumps of snow and the ground sparkling in the sudden light. Even the little fence post tops had caps of snow.

The driver stopped just short of the driveway. it didn't shut off, and whoever was driving kept the headlights on, too. Abel couldn't see what kind of vehicle it was from here, and the light gave him an instant headache when he looked too close. He toyed with the idea of shooting them out, then thought maybe that would be a waste of ammunition, depending on who, exactly, was here for a visit.

If it was law enforcement, if Quinn had somehow managed to get to a phone to call the cops...well, things were about to get interesting. That was a big if, he thought, so big that he wasn't even worried about it.

Two men stepped out past the lights and headed his way slowly, making their way through the snow with some effort. He stood up straight and went to greet them, coming down the stairs and walking their way. They would meet about halfway through the yard, far enough from the house that the men wouldn't see the condition of the door or the faint outline of Galloway's body. Abel thought that was good enough.

One of them raised a hand when he saw Abel so Abel blocked the direct light with a hand and tried to make out who was coming. Just barely he could see that the men didn't seem to be armed, the vehicle was a truck, and the truck had a circle logo on the door closest to him.

The power company. They were here to fix whatever had gone wrong with the electric lines.

"They got close enough to talk through the wind. "Still no power?" the one who had waved asked.

Take it easy, Abel thought, forcing his finger off the trigger of the rifle. He didn't lower it from his chest. "No sir. Phone's out too. Was hoping somebody called you fellas."

"No need - we've got sensors to tell us where the problems are."

The other man, the one who hadn't spoken yet, was looking past him toward the house. Or at least it looked that way. Since Abel couldn't see much more than their profile with the lights behind them like this, he wasn't sure. He stepped closer, angling his body to block the view. "Well, that's fancy."

"Yep. I just wanted you folks to know we were out here working, so we didn't spook you."

"Thanks for that." The tension in Abel's body made him want to scream, or punch somebody. He pushed down the urge. "I should let you men get to work."

"We shouldn't be long. It's a regular problem. We're pretty good at fixing this end of the line."

"I'll bet." Abel forced a chuckle and watched them walk away. His hands itched to raise the gun and fire, dropping them as they walked. He didn't need outside interference right now, not until he found Quinn and got her safely out of the way. What if she came back up the mountain using the road? She would walk right into them, and that would be a big problem.

Abel had already dragged the dog's body around to the barn, and he figured he had time before he needed to move Ethan's body. He had even considered waiting for Quinn. It was her husband, after all. He could make her help him with it. But if Quinn came back too soon, he would most likely have to kill both of the linemen. That'd be two more bodies.

Shit was starting to pile up.

He sat on the tops step, above Ethan Galloway's body, with the rifle across his knees. He watched them walk back to the truck and go to work. They backed the truck up a little, to get it closer to the pole they needed. One of the men, he couldn't tell which one, climbed into the bucket and it started to lift. The other man climbed out of the cab and went to watch him. Abel could see the faint outline of the bucket man's safety lines, and he wondered if he could aim well enough to shoot one. That got a chuckle out of him, but he knew damned well he was too tired to even consider that.

The drink was wearing off, too, which made him feel irritable and tired. He didn't plan on any of this, and bed was starting to sound like a pretty damned good idea, but now he had too much of a mess to clean up before he could think of sleeping. "No rest for the wicked," he muttered. Then he laughed, partly because the thought was funny and partly because who the hell said stuff like that in real life? It was just a bad...whatchamacallit...cliché.

The linemen's voices filtered out to him from time to time, but he didn't bother trying to listen. They were just working, getting the job done. He could admire that. For a moment he remembered what that felt like - to come home after an honest day's work and really relax, knowing he had done his job and done it as well as anybody could. It was a good feeling, but his last experience had been long enough ago that he barely remembered.

A stronger memory was the day he had walked away from that job, saying fuck it to everything that ever mattered to him. Right now, he couldn't remember what had set him off, but he knew it was bad. One of the problems with coasting through the days was forgetting things, and he'd been doing that a lot lately. Too much. He needed to get back on the horse, but every time he thought about it he just took another drink and turned his thoughts to something else.

The wind gusted hard against the side of his exposed face and he realized how cold he was, sitting here. He pushed up off the porch and shook himself. Then he looked down at the body under the snow, looked up again, at the men fifty yards away, and decided to go inside. The odds of them coming back over here were almost nonexistent. Why would they? They wanted to get home as soon as they could.

There was no need to sit here and guard a dead man.

He started to go into the house, then paused when he remembered the other reason he was out here - to make sure Quinn didn't come up the road, find the men working, and cause a fuss. He turned his head and looked that way, down toward Rick and Patty's place. It was damned dark, and he doubted he would see her coming anyway.

The wind kicked up again and one of the men let out a curse. Abel felt like it was burning his face.

Forget it. He was going inside. If the woman showed up, he'd deal with her then. He shot the linemen a salute that they couldn't see and stepped back through the front door.

It wasn't much warmer in here, and Abel thought it might help if he blocked the door. He wasn't sure how until he remembered how his Momma used to hang the blankets over the doorway to keep the heat in the main room of their house. Abel's bedroom would freeze, but the cold sure as hell got him out of bed in the mornings. He smiled at the memory and went to find a blanket.

He was just coming back from the bedroom with both arms full of comforter when the lights came back on. Good. That made the waiting a little easier, anyway. The linemen would leave, he could stoke up the fire and wait in comfort for Quinn to come on back home. He wasn't sure how he knew she was coming, but he knew it, sure as he knew his own name.

He was in the kitchen, headed for the front door, when he heard a loud thump and then a shout. It sounded like one of the linemen, but...dammit, it was way too close to the house.

He dropped the comforter on the kitchen counter and headed that way. When he went to the back of the house he had leaned the rifle against the recliner's arm, and now he grabbed it and kept going, through the room and out the door, not even slowing down.

When he stepped onto the porch, he stopped dead.

The lineman who had spoken to him earlier was standing at the bottom of the stairs, looking down at the body of Ethan Galloway. He was brushing off his hands, and it looked to Abel like the man had tripped over the corpse. The lights in and around the house blazed brightly, and when the lineman looked up his eyes were huge with fear and disbelief. "Dude!" he said. "There's a -."

Abel shot him in the head.

He watched the man fall like it happened in slow motion. At the same time, from somewhere farther off, he heard the other lineman yell. When the first one hit the bottom step and then the ground and lay still, he turned his attention that way.

The second lineman was down from the bucket, and now he yanked the passenger door open and tried to climb inside. He was wearing a set of coveralls that looked like the kind a mechanic wore in the winter. They were padded somewhat to protect from the cold, and that made his movements slow and imprecise. Abel stepped to the end of the porch and took aim.

The rifle clicked when he pulled the trigger. Damn it.

The second lineman was still fighting to get into the truck while Abel dug into his pants pocket for more ammo, while he loaded the gun and aimed it, and even when he took the shot. Of course, by now all he could see was the man's back, but that was enough. He fired, watched the coveralls jerk forward, saw the windshield turn red, and fired again.

The man stopped moving. Everything stopped moving. The sudden silence hurt Abel's head. He lowered the rifle, watched the two men for any sign of movement, and went back into the house to finish hanging his blanket.

The truck was going to be a problem, one he didn't feel like worrying about right now. He knew he should get rid of it, but there would be time enough for that later. If he left now, he might miss the big event - Quinn coming back.

In that regard, the truck might even help him out. She might see the truck, think help had arrived, and show her hand a little sooner than she otherwise would. She would walk right into his sights, and she wouldn't even know it until it was too late.

Chapter Eighteen

Quinn didn't bother looking for fresh clothes. She grabbed the coat from beside the door, called for Retro to stay by her side, and left the trailer.

Plunging back into the woods, she immediately felt exhausted. The drink had helped a little, but her adrenaline had used up all those helpful extra calories in a hurry.

She had toyed with the idea of taking the road back to her house - the terrain was a lot more forgiving - but she didn't want to run across Abel out in the open. If she was going to become the hunter, she was going to have to stalk him for a change and take him by surprise.

It was an odd feeling, this new strength she felt inside. Most of her was still in shock and praying that this whole night had just been a terrible dream, but other than that, she was driven by a small spark of anger. This was the Catch that she had avoided her whole life, since the moment she saw her baby brother's pale, slack face, and now it was staring her in the face.

She had seen what the Catch had done to her own mother, and she suspected that if she didn't face this thing on this night, the same thing would happen to her. She might survive, but she would waste the rest of her days hiding from the pain and waiting for somebody or something to come and fix what had gone so wrong.

The idea of it made her sick to her stomach, and she knew she could never let herself become that woman. If she didn't fight back now, she might as well walk up to Abel Welch and let him shoot her in the head. That would be a better fate than fading into the shadow her own mother had become.

So she went back into the woods, moving more deliberately than she had on the way down. She didn't want him knowing she was on her way. She didn't want to show her hand before she needed to in order to take him down. Most importantly, she had already decided that she needed to get to the barn before he noticed that she was back on the premises. She was going to need a weapon and she didn't dare hope that she could get to Ethan and the key without him seeing her.

She was halfway up the hill when she heard the gunshots.

Confused, she stopped mid-stride, with one hand firmly on Retro's neck. She felt his muscles vibrating under his fur as he fought hard to keep himself from barking. The woods were black as night, and she didn't dare turn on her flashlight, just in case. That gunshot probably meant that Abel was still at the house, but she couldn't be sure. It had sounded that far away, but these hills and hollows had a way of changing sounds. He could be just over the next rise, or he could be halfway down the main road - she just couldn't be sure enough to use the light and show her position.

The snow was coming down hard. She had noticed it when she stepped out of the trailer, but here under the trees it wasn't accumulating too quickly. She was still soaked, still cold, but at least she could follow her own trail back up the mountain.

She hoped with every painful step that she wasn't making a terrible mistake. She hoped that whatever god that existed was with her. She hoped that she could figure out a way to kill Abel Welch before he could kill her.

If that was even his plan. She hoped so, because the alternative would force her to take her own life, and that went against every instinct in her body. She wouldn't allow him to touch her, though, and she wouldn't allow him to take possession of the home she was building with Ethan. Those memories were too pure, too precious to let him ruin them.

She was breathing hard again by the time she topped the far side of the ravine and started down into the deepest part. Her chest hurt from a combination of exertion and tension. What would she find at home? She hadn't heard any more gunshots.

The fact that Burns hadn't found her by now told her that he was dead. That added to her hurt, because she knew that his death was her fault. She tried to remember that he had died for her, and he had died willingly, but that wasn't much comfort, especially when she noticed at odd moments that Retro would stop what he was doing and look around, like he missed his big brother. It broke her heart every time he did it and she tried to give him extra scratches, but she had more important things to do. "Just wait, boy," she told him, gasping a little,

"As soon as we get out of this I'll give you all the treats and the toys in the world. Maybe a new brother, too."

He panted up at her and turned his attention back to finding the way.

The clouds were finally breaking just a little, enough to let the moon shine blue across the snow but not enough to help her see all that much. The same tree cover that kept the bulk of the snow off her head also blocked the moonlight. If Abel was watching this way for her, that was a good thing, but it sure didn't help her navigate a safe trail. Once she got across the ravine, she had to slow down and watch her footing on every slope. More than once she slipped and landed on a knee or her butt. She climbed to the top wishing for a hot bath and a long night's sleep in her own bed.

She decided that she would get it, too, or die trying.

At the top of the ravine again, on the near side this time, she looked in the direction of the house but then turned away. Retro looked too. He even started that direction, but she didn't want him to do that. "Come on, boy," she said, patting her leg. "Let's go."

He ducked his head and followed.

She wondered if he could smell Burns from here. Did dogs know about death? Did they mourn?

She mentally mapped the house, land, and barns as she walked, making a plan. She didn't want to be scrambling when she finally faced Abel and she didn't want to be unarmed, either. She needed to move around for a little while without being seen. Going around the rear of the property, she would be able to sneak up to the barn without being seen, unless Abel was behind the barn waiting for her. She didn't think that was a possibility because it was so cold out, and the odds of her showing up here again were low. Why would she, since she'd already gotten away?

She wondered what the gunshots had been, then decided there was time enough to worry about that later. If she was lucky, Abel had killed himself, and all this work was for nothing. She didn't think she was lucky, though. *Better safe than sorry, Quinn.*

The land was flat behind the barn, but she still had to be careful. There was a lot of deadfall back here, branches and even whole trees that were too skinny or knotted for the loggers to pick up, and any one of them could trip her up and cause her to break her leg or arm if she fell wrong. She picked her way, kept

Retro close, and finally, just past the final line of trees she saw the wide field stretched out until it met the back of the barn.

It was dark against the white snow, but the lights inside shone brightly through the rear windows openings. She was glad she'd left them on for a moment, then changed her mind when she realized that the lights posed a problem.

If Abel looked toward the barn, he'd be able to see her moving around in there. She couldn't turn out the lights, either, because he would notice that, too.

Wouldn't he?

She paused at the edge of the field and watched for movement. When she spotted the white truck with the circle logo on it her heart began to race, but then she picked out more details and saw a leg hanging out of the passenger door. It wasn't moving. Underneath the foot, there was an irregular black spot. Blood.

That explained the gunshots and the lights.

The enormity of what Abel had done stole her breath, and instead of moving toward the barn, she sat down behind a tree a pulled her knees in, waiting for her heart to calm down.

Was he really planning to just kill anyone who came anywhere near the house? Was he that crazy? If so, she should just turn around right now and hike through the woods to the next mountain. Except that she was already running on fumes and with hungry coyotes on the move, she wasn't sure she'd even make it.

Besides, this was her home. No running, no whimpering in the shadows until help came. That could take a week. She needed to deal with Abel take back her home, and bury her husband.

Her husband, who was still probably laying where she left him. She wondered if he was completely covered with snow now. She thought about him being cold, and the idea of it nearly brought her to tears again.

Thinking about it brought her head up, as it dawned on her that that was why Abel had killed the lineman. The guy must have seen Ethan's body and figured out what was going on. He would have said something, for sure, and Abel couldn't just let him leave after that.

She got to her feet and checked the area again. Nothing was different, but the scene seemed even more ominous now that she knew - Abel was capable of killing purely innocent people. But why? She and Ethan had known their share of drunks before, and some of them had been deadbeats, living off others like Abel. None of them had ever killed people, though. Why was he doing it? What did he have to gain?

Surely he didn't believe he could just kill them and live in their home forever, like he owned the place. Somebody would eventually ask questions. She and Ethan tended to keep to themselves, but they had still made a few friends. Cap, for one, and his sister Mary. They came over on occasion. Was Abel going to kill them, too? Or the UPS guy who came about once a week when Ethan ordered something from Amazon?

None of this made any sense.

Then again, while none of the drunks they knew had killed anybody, they constantly made bad decisions and had a penchant for being overly optimistic. Maybe Abel did think he could just live here. Maybe he couldn't think so far ahead as to realize that it wasn't going to work.

The thought of him hurting anyone else dug at her. Not that she thought anyone would be out here tonight, but like the lineman, she couldn't know for sure. It was going to be up to her to stop Abel before he killed again.

The barn was a good five hundred yards from her, and there was plenty of open space in the field. She would have to depend on pure luck and speed to get her there without Abel glancing up at the wrong time and seeing her. Also, she was going to feel a gun trained on her heart the whole way, whether it actually was or not. Best to prepare her mind to ignore it now, before she got to the middle of the field and froze in fear.

She wasn't sure how she knew that, but she did. She wasn't the kind of woman who trained for this kind of thing, or even thought it could ever happen to her. There was nothing in her background, as far as she knew, that would help her here. And yet, she was operating on pure instinct, keeping her mind in check and not overthinking any of this. She could see it play out, see the pitfalls. She knew exactly which parts of her plan made her vulnerable and which parts required extra finesse.

She was going to have to trust her gut, and her gut seemed to know exactly what it was doing.

Just as she was about to step out into the open edge of the field, Retro lowered his head and growled. It wasn't loud - if she hadn't been so hyper aware right now, she might have missed it. She froze, her hand still on a clump of brush, about it push it aside.

She scanned the area as best she could, but didn't see anything different. No movement near the house, no change in the light. She glanced at Retro, and saw that he was looking away from the house, toward the road. She backed up a little and crouched beside him, ready to wait a minute.

When she finally realized what was going on, she sucked in her breath and held it.

It wasn't something moving that alarmed Retro. It was a sound. A sound she knew.

Cap was coming. The Gator was grinding up the mountain on the gravel road. She'd heard the sound of his engine enough to know it was him.

No. No, this wasn't the way. She had to stop this from happening.

There was only one way to do that. She paused for a second, took a deep breath, told Retro to stay, and broke through the trees, sprinting for the barn.

Chapter Nineteen

C ap wasn't sure, at first, if the Gator would make the climb. Even with the gravel the road didn't offer much in the way of traction, and more than once he had to back up and get a run at one slope or another. It was a little bit harrowing. More than once, he wondered if Mary was right about him wasting his time. More than once, he thought he wasn't going to make it.

When he got to the road that led to Ethan's cabin, he was surprised to see tired tracks. Somebody had come down off the mountain tonight. Cap didn't think it was Ethan or Quinn - both of their vehicles sported wider tires than these tracks indicated. This looked like a small car, or maybe stock dealer tires on a pickup. Cap couldn't think of anyone who could have made them.

He had stopped once to cover his face with a knit mask, trying to protect it from the wind. Even so, his hands and face were numb with cold, and his toes were starting to feel it through his heavy boots and thick socks. No matter. He hunched in and kept going, wrestling the Gator back into the road about every fifty yards or so.

The first sign of lights took him by surprise - usually the electric up here was the first to go. He had heard Ethan complain about it a hundred times, and he always laughed because he knew it was true. His own electric usually went out not long after, so he knew the drill. Maybe it had gone out - it was possible that the electric company had been here. That would explain the tire tracks, at least.

Now Cap thought that he really was wasting his time. If the electric company had been and gone, they would have called the police if anything was wrong, and they most likely wouldn't have left.

The Gator slid sideways, toward the drop-off, and interrupted his thoughts. He had to fight to get the machine stopped, and once he did he wasn't sure he could get it going again. Hell, he wasn't sure he wanted to - this was suicidal. At this rate, he was the one who would need help by the end of the night.

The thought made him chuckle to himself. Who would come out into this mess to help an old man? Everybody was most likely busy out toward town, towing the inevitable wrecks that always happened in weather like this. A tow truck would take hours to get here. If he was able, he'd have to walk to Ethan's for any kind of rescue.

He was glad that Mary hadn't come with him - for a minute there, he'd thought she was going to offer. The last thing he needed was an extra person to worry about. Himself, Ethan and Quinn were plenty, thank you very much.

Quinn, especially was an odd one. He knew from watching that she wasn't the kind of woman who was comfortable on a farm, and yet she had followed Ethan here willingly enough. Most women wouldn't do that. Then again, most women didn't look at their man the way she looked at Ethan. Like he was her axis or something. Like she couldn't live without him.

Not many marriages like that.

His own hadn't been like that, for a fact. He and Mercy June had been married less than two years before she died with the baby, and she'd spent every minute of those years complaining. She didn't like the mud. She didn't like the way he left her alone to go hunting. She didn't like church - her church at home had padded pews. She didn't even like the house he built for her. It was too dark, too narrow, too small. By the end, he agreed with her on that last part. Too small for the two of them, at least.

But then later, she was gone, and he regretted all the bickering. He regretted not paying more attention. If he had let her go back to the city, closer to her parents, would she be alive now? They certainly thought so. Barlow and Corliss Williams still hated his guts, after all these years. So much that they refused to come to Mercy's funeral and put a full page ad in all the local papers that accused him of killing her.

Which he hadn't. At the rate things were going, they might have killed each other, though. He chuckled at that. He was far enough away from the sadness now that he could feel lighter about it. Water under the bridge, he supposed. He'd made his peace.

After Mercy died, the house was a mess for a while. What with that and the ad in the paper, he took to staying inside. Even though folks he knew assured him that it was just the grief of distraught parents, he saw the way some of the younger kids looked at him. He took to avoiding town unless he had to go there, he stayed on the farm and worked on making it self-sufficient. He was getting pretty good at it, too, until his sister Mary called. She was sick, and she needed him.

That as it turned out, was enough. After all that time, Cap realized that being needed was what kept him going.

Now, maybe Ethan and Quinn needed him. Probably not, but then again, who wouldn't be touched that someone cared enough to come and check things out? Check on them? They would be gracious and sweet and invite him in to get warm, at the very least. Maybe Quinn would have a pie made.

He grinned under the icy mask, remembering the first time he'd met her. It had been just before Christmas, and she had their little cabin all dressed out with cedar wreaths and pretty lights on the tiny tree. She had just figured out how to make a pie crust, and she was as proud of that apple pie as any new mother. He'd been tickled at how tickled she was, and Ethan had stood by, beaming a little, while he tasted it.

It had been good pie. He told her so, and he thought she would bust wide open at the praise of an old man.

Kids. He liked to think his own would have been good people, like Ethan and Quinn. Since he didn't have any of his own, though, he'd adopted them instead.

The rear end of the Gator skidded out from under his butt, toward the ditch. He righted it without too much trouble. "Pay attention, old man, 'fore you end up in the creek down there."

When he saw the first twinkle of lights that told him he was close to the Galloway place, he slowed a little and started to feel somewhat foolish again. They were surely safe and sound. Ethan knew how to handle himself and protect his home. Cap knew for a fact that Ethan would do everything in his power to take good care of Quinn. Maybe he should turn around now and go on home. Let Mary laugh at his dumb ass, drink some coffee and go to bed where he could get warm.

But the thought of pie was a tease and the thought of heat was a promise, so he kept going. He would warm up and then go on home, hopefully without the gnawing feeling that something was wrong.

He spotted the utility truck, with its doors wide open, about the same time he heard the gunshot.

Chapter Twenty

Quinn spotted Abel about the same time he spotted her. She ducked behind the cedars, tried to stop there, and fell on her ass. What had caused her to...? Ethan's blood. It was all over the ground here, freezing. Just about the time she fell, one of the cedar's trunks splintered above her. If she had been standing she'd be dead. How in the hell was he such a good shot? He was a drunk, for crying out loud.

The thought brought her up short. He *was* a drunk, wasn't he? Now that she thought about it, she wasn't sure. He'd been drunk earlier in the night, when she had first encountered him, but that didn't necessarily mean he was a drunk. Another thing - the neighbors and their parties. It seemed to her that everyone who stayed with them tended to like the booze, but that wasn't definitive proof, either, was it?

She wished desperately that she knew what he wanted. Was it money? They didn't keep much in the house. Like the rest of America, they relied on debit cards and money transfers. Did he want to rape her?

Ew, gross. That thought gave her a shudder. It was possible, but she would kill him with her bare hands if he tried it.

Maybe he thought they had valuables in the house, but then why hadn't he just taken them and gone away?

She tossed the speculations aside and studied the path between her trees and the barn. It was a good hundred yards across wide open field, and now the moon was starting to brighten. Abel was standing at the top of the porch steps, watching for her. She could barely make out Ethan's body at the bottom, a shadow more than a solid person.

The last thing she wanted to do was make herself a sitting duck, but Cap was coming. He was going to walk right into this mess, completely unaware of Abel. He could be dead before he knew what was happening.

She was studying the field between her and the barn, looking for potential problems, when she caught movement from her right.

Abel saw it too. She noted the flash of light on black metal as he swung the rifle that way. When she looked, her heart sank.

Retro was heading her way, running across the snowy field so fast that it looked like he was flying.

She saw Abel raise the rifle, saw him take aim. She didn't see his hand move, but she saw him lower the rifle and look at it with his head cocked.

Something had gone wrong. Maybe the gun had jammed. Thank God.

Retro almost knocked her over before he could get stopped. He tried so hard to miss her that he slipped in the blood, too, and fell sideways, skimming across the ground and smacking his big dumb head against the cedar trunk next to hers. He yelped a little, but she wasn't sure if it was a yelp of surprise or pain.

But he got up and shook himself, then came to her. She wasn't supposed to love on him when he disobeyed, but she reached down and scratched his ears anyway. She was glad to see him alive. He panted up at her but then returned his attention to the house and started to growl.

Abel was still fiddling with the gun. She didn't know what had happened, but she sent a silent prayer of thanks skyward. For the first time since this nightmare had started, she felt like God had given her a bit of a break. Retro was still alive.

She searched the other direction, toward the road, but saw no sign of Cap. Had he stopped somewhere? She strained to listen for the Gator's engine and heard nothing but the wind and Retro's breathing. She knew she'd heard it, though, and if she could hear it, Abel could too. He would figure out what was wrong with the gun, fix it, and go investigate.

Unless she distracted him. She didn't want to leave the safety of the trees, but it might be the only way to keep Cap safe. He was too old to be running through the woods, too old to die cold and alone by the side of the road. She would never forgive herself if something happened to him. With a curse, she turned back to Abel. She needed to distract him.

More than anything, she hated that he had the upper hand here. She should be able to walk back into her house, take a shower, and go to bed in peace. But she couldn't. Instead, she was soaked and freezing in the snowy dark, possibly about to die or cause the death of someone she cared about.

Or both. There was no skirting around the fact that Abel was one trigger-happy son of a bitch.

If she was smart she would just run. Plunge into the trees behind her, travel through the woods until she got the Cap, wherever he was now, and leave all of this behind.

But she didn't want to leave Ethan and she didn't want to leave her home. "No turning back now, Quinn," she muttered to herself. Then, with her heart in her throat, she stepped out from behind the tree and started walking toward the house.

A million thoughts filled her head, but over all of it was pure raw fear, screaming for her to turn back.

She couldn't. Not with Cap's life in the balance.

She saw Abel glance up from the rifle and bend down again. Then he did a double take, which might have been funny under different circumstances. He straightened and watched her come.

Her mind raced, trying to figure out what she was going to do when she got to the house. She doubted she could match him in hand to hand fighting, and her weapons were so limited that it was laughable. But above it all, one thought kept thrumming through her head - this was her home, and her husband, and this man named Abel was trespassing.

She was within twenty feet of him, about to speak, when she heard the one thing she didn't want to hear: pounding paw beats, coming up behind her fast. Retro. Before she even completed the thought, Retro was past her, going at a dead run. She saw him flash by, saw Abel shift his attention. His expression - she was close enough to see it now - changed from malicious triumph to surprise and then fear. His arm came up, but Retro was already on him, sinking strong teeth into Abel's coat sleeve.

Quinn heard Abel cry out, heard him grunting with effort. She saw Retro climb on top of the man and heard his teeth snapping as he worked to get his jaws around something more substantial than fabric. She called his name, barely hearing her own voice.

She started to run. One wrong move and Abel would kill Retro, either by snapping his neck or -.

Retro yowled, heaved, and rolled away. He lay still.

Just like that, she saw the last of her family slip away. She felt her heart break. She didn't stop running. She ran faster. When she got to where Retro lay in the darkening snow, she fell to her knees and buried her face in his fur.

"Retro!" The name slipped out. She shook him. She grabbed his big head with both hands and turned his face to hers.

His eyes focused on her and then the recognition faded. He was dying. His ribs, when she slid her hands along them, barely rose and fell, and there were hitches in the rhythm as he struggled to live.

"Retro, baby," she moaned. "Please, Retro, I need you, buddy."

He whined at her, but he couldn't lift his head.

Nearby, closer to the porch, Abel fought his way up out of the snow. When he was standing, he brushed off his coat. "Damned dog," he muttered.

Then he knelt again and started feeling around.

He'd lost the rifle in the snow.

She wanted to die, too. Within sight of her, she could see the bodies of her dog, her husband and a stranger. No wait - she peered at the steps. Two strangers. She didn't know who it was, and she couldn't bring herself to care. Laying Retro's head gently down, she stood up and walked away, toward the woods.

Abel had given up on finding the rifle, apparently. He stood up, tuned and lunged at her. She rolled away, onto her back and scrambled backward, out of his reach. He landed hard on his shoulder. She heard him grunt. He got up and clambered after her, but now she was out of reach. She saw him try to stand, pushing up on his hands, but then he hissed and fell again. "Mother -," he snapped.

He had hurt himself. Good.

She stood up and walked away, toward the woods.

The glistening field stretched out to the trees, but she barely noticed. She didn't want to be here, didn't want to keep going. She was tired, and she fully expected Abel to find his rifle and shoot her in the back before she got to the cover of trees.

The glistening field stretched out to the trees, but she barely noticed. She didn't want to be here, didn't want to keep going. She was tired, and she fully expected Abel to find his rifle and shoot her in the back before she got to the cover of trees.

In a way, she welcomed it. What could be worse than what had already been done to her. If her heart stopped beating, it would stop hurting, right? No more fear, no more sadness. Just maybe, finally, peace. She'd spent nearly her whole life, in retrospect, waiting for the other shoe to drop. She didn't know how or where or why, but she'd always known that the Catch was right around the corner, and now here it was. It was almost a relief, the way it happened. No long slow slide into depression, watching Ethan slowly fall apart before her eyes. No more growing old, waiting for her eyes to go, her organs to give out, or any of the other horrible things that happened in the later years. After all of that, there was only death. Not a strong argument for her to keep fighting for some semblance of life. At the moment, that was all she wanted. She thought it would be relaxing at this point, after the night she had.

But she reached the tree line and stepped inside with no loud boom, no searing pain in her spine, no sound at all. Was he just watching her leave, or was he still scrambling for the gun? Why didn't he chase her, at least?

The woods were black as a mine, but she didn't bother getting out her light. Who cared if she didn't make it far? Abel would come to his senses and come after her in a minute anyway. What was she going to do about that? She stubbed her foot on a stump, caught her balance, and kept walking. This way would lead her to the main road, at least.

And, now that she thought about it, where was Cap? She knew she had heard the Gator, but he hadn't shown up.

Maybe he heard the gunshot. That was probably it. He had turned around and left, and she blew out her breath in relief when the thought occurred to her. Good. The last thing she needed was another person to worry about.

At the rate Abel was going, he'd dropped half the population of the county tonight. And she still didn't know his motivation. She still didn't understand how things had spiraled so out of control so quickly. She had woken up this morning a happily married woman with pets and chickens and a whole new day stretching out in front of her.

Now she was lost, in the dark and the snow. Cold, alone, heartbroken and probably not going to survive the night.

Truth be told, she didn't even care.

A low growl interrupted her thoughts and brought her head up. Yellow eyes blinked all around her. She stumbled to a halt, but the eyes weren't as still. Several of them moved, slowly weaving through the trees toward her, an inch at a time. She stopped walking and backed up a little, trying to make sense of what she was seeing.

Then it hit her. Coyotes.

They were hungry this time of year, and she had already interrupted one of their meals tonight. In a way, it was fitting, wasn't it? The circle of life and all that.

This wasn't the way she wanted to die.

She very carefully felt for footing with her heels, trying to back away. If she fell right now, she'd be dead. Coyotes wouldn't give her time to get up and start moving again. They would be on top of her in an instant, tearing out her throat. She thought of those nature documentaries that Ethan liked to watch and shuddered. Abel's bullet in her back was a better alternative.

Her shoulder caught a tree trunk and stopped her. The eyes, reflecting the dim light of the house behind her, kept coming. She could see glimpses of ragged gray fur.

She slumped against the tree. Her mind was skimming through ideas to get her out of danger, but her body felt heavy and raw. She couldn't move any more. She couldn't even think of how to move. Get behind the tree? Try to climb it? Run? Her feet weren't cooperating. It was like she was nailed here, in the place she would die.

Her heart ached for everything she had lost. And it had all happened on one day, in a mad dash of a few hours. The only thing left was her life, and there were only a few minutes of it left.

It was a relief, in a way. She imagined it was like child birth - incredible pain, but always an eventual end in sight. At least she could rest.

But wasn't death just another kind of hiding? A permanent surrender? She felt something close to shame underneath her exhaustion, and it pierced her chest as surely as a bullet.

She swiped at her face and realized that she was crying. Well, that was a logical reaction to this sort of thing. Besides, she didn't have the energy to fight the tears back anymore. She let them fall.

The coyotes were close enough now that she could smell the stink on their fur. She had always heard that predator animals - coyotes, bears, big cats - had a stink from the dead meat of their diet, but she never imagined that it was this bad. She tried blowing the smell out of her nostrils, but it didn't work, and the thought of breathing through her mouth made her sick to her stomach.

They were within a few feet from her now. She turned her head away. A small, pathetic noise rose unbidden from her throat when she imagined teeth sinking into her flesh. She imagined that she could feel their breath on her now, even though that was impossible. They weren't close enough.

Yet.

Hiding again. That's what she was doing. Hiding. Running away. She wasn't even physically willing to face her own death.

Hiding away, like her mother did all those years ago. The end result would be quicker, but the result was the same.

Ethan would be so disappointed.

That last thought nearly stole her breath away. Ethan, the one person on earth who was important to her, who was a part of her, had always encouraged her to be stronger than her past. He had talked her through all the trauma of that birthday afternoon so long ago. He had been her comfort and her protector. Even in death, she knew that he was protecting her from the pain of watching him slowly fall apart.

If she gave up now, his death would mean nothing.

Almost involuntarily, her hands felt behind her back for the rough trunk of the tree. If she could climb it, she could get away from these animals and figure out what to do.

The bravest of the coyotes was too close now. She was going to have to take a chance.

Just as she worked up her nerve to turn around and try to shimmy up the tree, the coyote jumped at her. She cried out and spun away, hanging onto the trunk but putting it between her and those teeth.

It worked for the moment, the coyote smacked against the wood and fell back, but he was already sinking into a crouch, ready to try again. Another of the coyotes was following suit, coming closer. She backed up.

And fell. Her heel dropped onto something that rolled under her step and brought her down onto her side. There was a rush of noise - the coyotes were seizing their advantage. She covered her head with her hands and hoped Ethan could forgive her.

A new sound made everything stop. She heard it, but she didn't know what it was. Sharp, short...it sounded like...

A gunshot.

She slowly raised her head. The coyotes were gone, the last of them flashing gray fur between the trees.

"Get up."

Cap stepped out from behind a tree. She scrambled to her feet, remembering hearing the Gator's engine. She realized that it had stopped somewhere along the road, before it got to the house. "Cap?" She rushed at him, the cold chill of her imminent death melting into the warmth of recognition. She was awash with relief. "Thank God you're here."

He patted her shoulder awkwardly, but let her hug him. "Just about got you, didn't they?" he asked.

She stepped back, shivering now that her adrenaline rush was wearing off. "Why are you here? In the woods, I mean? I heard your Gator, but..."

He shook his head and pulled up his coat tail to holster a small pistol. She hadn't noticed it before right now. "Cap, don't put that away."

He stopped. "Why? What's happening?"

"There is a man at my house. He killed the dogs, Cap. He's broken in and I don't know what to -."

"Where is Ethan?" Cap put a hand on her arm and gave her a little shake. "Quinn, where is Ethan?"

She took a deep breath. For the first time, she said it out loud. "He's dead, Cap."

The words tore through her and her knees threatened to buckle under her weight. Her voice sounded far away and wrong, somehow, like she was lying to him. She wasn't, though. There was no doubt that Ethan was in fact dead, along with Burns and Retro. Her whole life, every member of her family, had been ripped out of her hands in a few hours. How did a person come to terms with something like that? How did a human heart survive it?

She didn't know, but she was sure of one thing now - she would survive this, because Ethan had given his life for it. He hadn't wanted to hold her back, or wear her down with the needs he saw coming.

Her resolve, shaky and thin, was still there. "Cap, I need your gun."

Chapter Twenty-One

Abel watched Quinn disappear into the darkness, but when he pushed up from the ground his wrist gave way and flattened him again, practically burying him in snow. He had landed wrong on one of the paving stones, twisting his wrist and cracking a kneecap hard. It probably wouldn't have stopped him, but the cold made everything ten times worse. He didn't want her to get away. It was damned cold out here. He wanted her inside and secured, so that he could fix the stupid door and warm up the house.

He was going to need to go soon. If he couldn't catch up with her in the next few minutes, he knew she would get to the main road and help. Someone would come, maybe the police, and if he was here when they showed up it was all over.

Of course, if he could catch her before she got there, well, everything might work out all right.

He was hurting. And tired. God he was tired. The liquid courage was wearing off and he wanted to sleep for days. He'd sure as blown that option, hadn't he? He wanted to chuckle at his own stupidity, but his lungs were starting to hurt. He should go back inside out of the weather for a bit, but she wasn't going to give him that luxury.

He finally got to his feet, but he was still funny headed and swaying a little. It didn't matter. He was going to stop her, because the other option ended with him back in prison, and he'd turn the gun on himself before he'd do that.

Like Ethan Galloway here. He wondered what transgression Galloway had committed that he couldn't face the consequences. Probably something stupid. Rich guys always ended up doing something stupid and then getting caught.

Or...there was the slim possibility that Abel was getting it all wrong. He wasn't a detective. For all he knew, Quinn had killed poor old Ethan and made it look like a suicide. He doubted it, though. If she had the balls to kill a man, she would have killed him by now.

Wouldn't she? Maybe she didn't have the guts, but Ethan had driven her to it. The guy was prissy, and Abel couldn't imagine any woman putting up with that for too long.

What she needed was a steady hand to keep her in line. Abel didn't think Ethan was that kind of guy. He was more of a sweater wearing-book reading man who rarely looked up to see what his wife was doing. That didn't make any sense to Abel - why have a wife if you didn't care what she did? Wives could cause a fair amount of trouble, and they needed to be leashed a little.

Abel started toward the woods, but then something told him to stay away. The woods were a no-go, because of the dark and because of his wounds.

He needed to bring Quinn to him, but he didn't think she was smart enough to fall for just anything.

He looked around. Everything she loved was dead, so she must be just about broken now. It wouldn't take much...

He did a full one-eighty and looked at the house. Then he grinned.

There was one thing a woman seemed to need, more than anything else. Abel didn't understand it, but then he wasn't a woman. He considered it one of their weaknesses, and it was a weakness he had no trouble using to his own advantage. He glanced at the woods one more time and headed for the back of the house.

It wasn't hard to do - a little straw from the chickens, a kicked out post or two from the dog pen. He put down the rifle, assembled his new supplies, and dug a lighter from his pocket.

Abel knew what he was doing, but he also knew what it *looked like* he was doing, and that was the beauty of the plan. Quinn would see one thing and one thing only - the destruction of her very last and most important possession.

She'd come running, and then he could get his hands on her.

Did he want her? For a while. He could have some fun, but then she would have to go. This was his home, and he didn't think Quinn Galloway would be a suitable mate for him. She was too uppity. She probably couldn't even cook.

The fire caught quick and heat bloomed up around his face. He went to get more straw, because straw would create a lot of smoke, which he needed to draw her out. He wished he had an old tire or two - they created huge, scary clouds of smoke.

But he didn't, so he shooed the chickens out of the way and gathered as much straw as he could, still favoring his injuries but excited now and ready to end this thing. It had gone on for too long. The snow was falling thickly enough that he had to blink it away a few times, but he didn't slow down. The promise of a warm bed tempted him too much. He didn't even care if she was in it with him or not.

There was another problem, though he wasn't too worried about it. Just before he spotted her running from the woods behind the barn, Abel was sure he had heard the sound of an engine. It was faint, but the way she took off the minute he noticed it made him think it wasn't his imagination. But who would come up this road in these conditions and then just stop before they got here. Abel knew Quinn hadn't called anyone - she hadn't been in the house since the beginning of all this.

The fire crackled sharply in the steaming air, throwing up sparks like dust. He leaned in, hoping to warm his bones while he waited.

It might take a few minutes, but he knew she was watching and he knew she would come. She didn't have a choice.

The night was dark, away from the campfire, and he wondered if he would be out here, enjoying the fire, if his life had turned out differently. Would he be here with a woman he loved? Would he have a good job or a clean record? Maybe he's be in the Rotary Club or own his own successful business in town. He chuckled at that, wondering what kind of business a guy like him would open.

Maybe a liquor store. He chuckled again and shoved his hands deeper into his pockets. Then he walked to the corner of the house, where he could see the tree line, and watched for Quinn to come.

What if she didn't? What if he misjudged how much she cared about this place? She might say, "Good riddance," throw her hands up, and walk away.

To where, though? Where was she going to go? It was dark and snowing and the terrain was difficult. She would be dead before she made it to the main road, especially if she got off track. Between the predators, the weather, and her own fear, she was certain to get lost long before she got help.

His toes were starting to hurt. He shuffled his feet to get them warm. First thing after he got access to the Galloway money, he was going to buy a new pair of boots. It was only fair - he'd got blood all over these anyway, thanks to the husband.

And that was part of it, wasn't it? He wasn't going to let her go. He was going to take possession of the life he deserved, even if it ended up with Quinn Galloway at the bottom of one of these ravines. And honestly, how else could it possibly end?

Chapter Twenty-Two

Quinn was looking at Cap like he owed her. "Give me your gun," she said again.

Cap hesitated, but then handed over the small .22 pistol that had belonged to his father, and his father before him. It was cold enough against his bare palm that for a minute he thought it would stick and hurt when she took it. Even in this glimmering unlit night, he knew she meant business. He could feel it, rolling off her like heat. He wondered how many men that pistol had killed and then he wondered if it would kill one more man tonight. From the way she squeezed his wrist before taking the gun, he thought it probably would.

She took the gun and asked if it was loaded. He nodded once, yes.

He hadn't thought he would need the weapon. He had only put it into the Gator's Tuff Box out of habit. Too many times he'd caught himself up against a snake or a fox without the reassurance of some sort of defense, so he'd started carrying it with him. Going on fifteen years now, and he'd only needed it a handful of times. He'd most likely retire it after tonight. If he ever got it back.

She hunched her shoulders and he realized that she had to be freezing. "Here," he said, reaching for the zipper of his coat.

She shook her head. "No, Cap. You'll get sick." She pointed her free finger. "And don't you dare follow me. I got this."

Then she turned and walked away, back through the woods. He started to follow her anyway, but the falling snow obscured her from sight within seconds. He didn't know what she was planning, but he thought it best to stay out of the way and listen.

Still, he started making his way through the woods.

He was nearly to the tree line, and the house lights were in sight again, when two things happened. First, he saw the smoke. It curled high in the air above the house, thick and pale compared to the night around it. Second, he was so busy looking for Quinn's form that he didn't pay attention to where he stepped.

One broken branch, one wrong move, and something snapped, right before the pain in his leg took him to his knees and then his face. He yelled and got a mouthful of snow. Then he rolled over and grabbed his calf, curling his limbs together like some giant unshaven praying mantis. He swallowed his moaning because he didn't want Quinn to worry, if she could even hear. Then he rolled to a gnarled pine and tried to stand.

The pain in his leg shot through the rest of his body and he hissed, sliding back down the trunk to the ground. It took a good ten minutes before he was able to unclench his jaw and open his teary eyes again.

When he did, he saw several pairs of eyes staring back at him. They were maybe a hundred yards away.

Dupree Captin took a long hard look at them, counted off five coyotes altogether, and started to pray.

He prayed for his soul, and then he prayed for Mary. He prayed for salvation, forgiveness and retribution, not necessarily in that order. Finally he prayed for Quinn and her husband, and for his God to strengthen her as she battled the degenerate that had taken her house.

He prayed for a long time, but he never closed his eyes.

Chapter Twenty-Three

Quinn felt Cap's eyes on her as she made her way toward the house, but she didn't turn around and go back.

Even though she wanted to. Even though a large part of her mind thought that she was on a suicide mission. But her mind wasn't in charge right now. It felt to her like her thoughts had taken a firm backseat to her feelings.

And her feelings wanted revenge. Her feelings wanted to do something, to take back what was hers. It was an ancient thing, this raw anger that welled inside of her. She knew that her emotions echoed the emotions of millions of others, down through the ages, who felt the same and sometimes succeeded. She carried the gun pointed toward the ground, beside her leg. It was surprisingly light, considering the heaviness of the work ahead.

For that matter, she somehow felt light as well. Her belly curled in nervous anticipation, but not fear. She was beyond afraid, she thought, as if the decision to do something had erased her overriding need for self-preservation.

Would she die tonight? Probably.

Did she care? Yes, she did, although the caring seemed small and far away. If she didn't, would it matter?

If she did, would that matter?

She kept her eyes on the house lights and moved between the trees, watching for any sign of where Abel Welch was waiting. She saw the vehicles off to her left, and then the porch. At the bottom of the porch lay her husband and ...

She pulled her eyes away.

She could only see part of the back yard from here - the chicken house and a corner of the dog pen. The barn was farther back, closer to the trees.

An eerie yellow light flickered to life against the snow. She stared at it, curious, but then she saw the smoke.

Rage blinded her for a moment, and then her vision cleared and she started to run, pulling the pistol up as she went and clicking off the safety.

She'd been wrong - he still had the power to rip something from her. Her home. And now he was doing it.

This night should have been like any other. She and Ethan should have been snuggled together inside, making a home-made pizza or eating his world famous potato soup. They should have been comfy and warm, happy and secure in the knowledge that the stars were above, the snow was fine and pretty, and the world was turning as it should. Their island of wonderful solitude had become an isolation cell in the cruelest prison, and the jailer was a sadistic mother-fucker.

This monster had come out of nowhere, striking at her most vulnerable moment, and then ground his heel into her life. For what? Why was he doing this? What did he stand to gain, and when would this night of horrors end?

She broke through to the open field and headed for the driveway, skirting around the front of the cabin to avoid falling apart when she saw Ethan's still and silent body. And Retro, her sweet boy, who had given his life to save hers.

She let the rage rip through her, white hot and beating brute wings inside her chest. Her heartbeats blended with her footfalls as she got to the other end of the house and crouched just beyond the light.

She wanted to see. Abel couldn't be inside the burning house, unless he had decided to end this on his own terms. She was surprised to find that the thought made her even angrier. She wanted to kill him. She wanted to watch him die and dance around his lifeless body.

The shadows were wrong.

That was the first thing she noticed. The angle of the shadows was all wrong for the situation. They should have been flickering directly to the west, toward the ravine and the river, but they weren't it was almost like the old barn was on fire instead.

But that wasn't exactly right, either...

She stood slowly and started walking again, away from the house a little way, aiming to come in behind the dog pen for cover. It would take some care and some stealth, but she thought that if she curbed her rushing anger and took care to watch her surroundings, she could get there in one piece.

She was going to have to stop and rest soon, but feeling safe enough to do that might take years of work, and there was no chance in hell of it happening while Abel Welch still walked free.

She thought about the blood on the cabinet at the neighbor's house. Was it human? Did it belong to someone in that house? She doubted that it was Abel's, so it had to belong to someone. Rick? Patty? One of the kids? The thought turned her stomach.

It didn't matter. None of it mattered but the next few moments, when either her or Abel would bleed out in the snow.

She gauged her distance from the soft edge of the yellow lights and kept away from it until she was fully behind the dog pen. Crouched there, with a hand over her mouth to help dissipate the white plume of her breath, she saw the reason for her confusion.

The house wasn't on fire. Her shoulders dropped, and she almost laughed out loud. No wonder the fire hadn't grown out of control while she moved. No wonder Abel wasn't scuttling out of the house like a cockroach. He wasn't in the house - he was behind it, feeding a small but smoky fire.

He was trying to flush her out.

The woods where Cap waited was behind him now, beyond the reach of the firelight. She could see his face clearly for the first time, and she wasn't surprised that his thin frame, wracked with the ravages that years of drinking brought, matched the hollowed, scruffy cheeks of his visage. He reminded her of old pictures she'd seen - mine workers from the turn of the century, who carried shovels as tall as them and wore baggy clothes with mostly dirt holding them together.

Her hand clutched the pistol's metal grip and itched to move, to come up, aim, and blow the small man's brains out.

A coyote howled, close enough to raise goose bumps on her scalp. She paused. That sounded like it was coming from where Cap was hidden.

She looked that way, then glanced at Abel again. A sinking feeling soured her gut.

Cap was unarmed. He might need her.

If it wasn't already too late.

She wanted to fire on Abel and then run to Cap, but what if she missed? What if her bullet went wide, leaving him to fire back and take her down, leaving Cap alone to fight off a group of coyotes.

She knew she was assuming a lot of things - that the coyotes were on Cap, that he was unarmed, that she would miss, that Abel actually wanted to kill her instead of...worse. It was a long list, but one thing she didn't assume on this night was that her luck hadn't run out. It obviously had, and now she had a few important choices to make. Life or death choices.

Satisfy her revenge, or go to Cap and ensure his safety, maybe at the expense of her own.

She watched Abel go to the hen house, step inside the enclosure, and bend down. He was gathering more straw, hoping to build up the smoke and bring her running to save her house.

As she watched she realized something. She had wanted to save her house, it had seemed like the last, most important thing in her life until right now.

Right now, Cap was more important.

She backed away from the dog pen as quietly as she could, while Abel was busy with the fire. When she reached the dark again, she turned and started to make her way back toward the woods.

She was almost there, just a few more feet across the last open part, when she heard something that spun her around.

A bark.

Retro.

Joy shot through her, but then died again when Abel appeared at the corner of the house. She saw his head swivel her way. Saw it stop. He shifted the raised rifle and aimed it at her chest. "Hey, bitch," he called.

Quinn stepped backward, toward the woods.

Froze.

Swallowed hard. Her breath hitched. Her chest ached.

She wanted to look away, toward the woods where Cap was possibly in trouble, but the barrel of the rifle, even from a good five hundred yards away, mesmerized her. It was such a simple thing, steel and long, no adornment or complexity at all. And yet it could end her as surely as this night would end.

Retro was struggling to get up, but he couldn't. He barked again. She winced and willed him to be quiet, before Abel turned and put a bullet into his head. Miraculously, he stilled.

She couldn't judge the distance, couldn't tell if she had time to run. Her mind was calculating where to step, when to run, whether to duck...but her body refused to do anything at all. She might have been rooted to the spot forever if not for one thing.

Very faintly, through the soft weight of falling snow, she heard Cap's voice. No words, either she wasn't close enough to make them out or the snow muffled them. But his voice, small and far, startled her.

Abel still stood at the edge of the house, in front of the fire. It made him seem like a demon that had finally shed any attempt at humanity. The flames licked up from behind him, painting him black, and yet Quinn could make out his features just enough to see that he was grinning.

The man was crazy. He didn't want anything at all, except to tear through her life and cause all the heartache he could manage, regardless of who she was or what his eventual punishment might be.

The flames painted the snow red, and yet closer to her, the flat width of the yard sparkled a cool blue in the partial moonlight. She wasn't cold, or hot, or afraid anymore. She simply was, still and small under the frozen sky, her heart beating too fast, her breath rising in front of her eyes.

And as she looked at Abel standing between her and her home, something snapped into place. He was the Catch. He was the other shoe, the doom she'd been waiting for all these years. The terrible surprise that Ethan had been trying so hard to protect her from, that she'd been hiding from since she could remember. He was it, and it was here.

In spite of the fear and the dread, a sweeping sense of pure relief swept through her.

All these years, she had imagined an overwhelming monster, but now she saw that the worst thing was always in her imagination. Her own mind had built up the crushing catastrophe that she always feared, and now that she was faced with it she knew that most of the nightmare was inside her.

She stared at him for a moment longer, more curious than anything, and then she raised the pistol and fired off a shot in his general direction. She felt calm, almost dreamlike. She watched him duck away, behind the house. Then she turned her back on him and walked into the woods.

The house could wait. Abel could wait. Cap needed her.

Once she got past the tree line, she broke into a run, calling for him. Tree branches scratched at her arms, and the uneven ground tried to trip her up a few times. When she saw him, he was backed hard against a tree trunk, holding his leg. "Cap?"

Movement all around made her turn to see, and she caught sight of gray fur, moving through the trees. Away.

"Coyotes," he said. His voice was ragged. "Don't you ever take my gun again."

"I'm sorry." She glanced at his leg. "What happened?"

"I think I broke it. Pretty sure I broke it."

She sank to her knees and moved his hand. His ankle was swelling fast. It was purple and dark under the glow of the flashlight. "You can't stand on it, can you?"

He shook his head, lips tight against the pain. She wanted to hug him, but they were in trouble. She needed to think. "How do I get you back to the Gator without hurting you?" she asked.

He shook his head and barked a laugh. "Slowly."

She glanced back the way she had come, toward the house, trying to guess how much time she had before Abel decided to try something new.

"Don't worry about me," he said. "You scared off the coyotes, that's good enough."

She wanted to believe him. The driving urge to end this mess was pulling at her. But she knew he wouldn't last long out in this cold and wet. Oh, she might be able to get him home, but she knew that, left out in the elements for so long, he would end up sick. At his age, sick was dangerous.

She couldn't stand the thought of any more death tonight.

"Cap," she said, making up her mind. "Shut up. I'm going to help you up and get you back to the Gator now. All right?"

He laughed again, but there was pain in it. "All right."

It took some shoving and tugging and pulling, but she got him to his feet. Then he reached to prop himself on the nearest tree trunk. "I think I can ride the trees all the way back to the road, with your help," he said, testing his weight on his hurt leg, wincing, and shaking his head. "Definitely need your help."

"No problem, Cap. I'm right here with you."

She wanted to thank him and tell him how grateful she was that he had come out here to check on her. She wanted to tell him that it meant something, that his actions - which he most likely thought were a small thing - meant more to her than he would ever know. But there would be time for all that later. Right now, she wanted to concentrate on getting him to safety.

She got under his arm, staggering a bit before she got her footing, but then righting herself. "Ready?" she asked.

He glanced back over his shoulder, searching. Maybe for the coyotes, she thought. Maybe not. "I suppose," he said. "We don't have to do this right now."

She cut him off. "Hush, please. I need to listen."

He nodded and started off. She kept up, hoisting maybe twenty five percent of his weight with every step. Every time he stopped to breathe, she listened and waited for the sound of Abel sneaking up behind them, or the soft padding of feet that would warn her the coyotes were back.

"Who is it?" Cap asked at one point, after they had gone a little way.

Quinn shook her head. "Not sure. His name is Abel Welch. I think he's been staying with the neighbors down by the river."

Cap grunted but didn't respond to that. Instead he said, "You need to come with me. Leave now. We'll call the police."

She looked away, out toward the darkness of the woods. He was right - she should leave now while she had the chance.

But something told her that it was the wrong thing to do. No - that wasn't right. It was the correct thing to do, but she couldn't bring herself to do it.

If Abel was her Catch, then she needed to face him. Otherwise...well, otherwise, she would spend the rest of her life, no matter where she ended up, looking for the next something bad to slink out of the shadows. And when it did, finally, it would devour her, because walking away now would highlight how weak she felt. In fact, every time a Catch showed up, she would remember her running on this night and run again.

She had been running and hiding since she was a child. That wasn't how she wanted to spend the rest of her life. It wasn't how Ethan would want her to spend the rest of her life. He had made her strong, and running away would insult his memory. Instead of trying to explain it all to Cap, she just shook her head.

He let it go with a quiet, knowing nod.

"Ethan was developing Alzheimer's," she said. "He killed himself."

Cap was quiet, working his way to the next tree. Listening.

"He didn't want me to live with that. You know, taking care of him, dealing with all the heartache."

"The Gator is right up here," he said.

She didn't answer, but helped him along. She could see the red tailgate of the machine, just off the main road.

"He made the right choice," Cap said.

That hurt. "I don't think so."

"I know. But he did. You wouldn't understand how a man sees weakness."

"No, Cap. Ethan wasn't like that. He wasn't some macho guy who had to prove how tough he was."

Cap grunted. "We all are, deep down, Quinn."

She didn't think so, but she wasn't about to argue.

The sharp crack of a broken branch made her gasp and half turn.

"Quinn Galloway."

She stared at Abel Welch, wide-eyed. She had hoped she could hear him coming, hoped he would take his time. Long enough for her to get Cap out of harm's way.

Cap squeezed her shoulder with his arm and then let go of her. She turned to face Abel.

He was holding the rifle, but he was aiming it at Cap's head.

Quinn didn't wait, didn't think. She threw herself at him, knocking him backward. She landed on top of him in the knee-deep snow and started hitting. And hitting, and hitting. She didn't know where her fists were landing, and she didn't care. She was so tired of him, of this night, of a lifetime of fear, that all she wanted to do was make it stop. If she had to pummel him to death with her bare hands, she had to make it stop.

Everything was a blur. Her knuckles hurt every time she connected with his head or arm or chest. She didn't give him even a moment to retaliate, because she knew that if she did it was all over. He would overpower her easily, kill Cap, and do whatever the hell he was trying to do. Maybe she would die. Maybe worse. She couldn't fathom his intentions, and she didn't care to. She just knew that she needed to end this thing, and end it now, before he ended her. She burned with the fury of all her pain.

Chapter Twenty-Four

A bel didn't expect the woman to attack him, so he wasn't prepared to throw up his hands and stop her. If he were on his feet it would be easy, but his heel had bashed against something and taken him down when she launched herself at his chest. Now all he could do was roll around, trying to get out from under her, and maybe get his hands between them to push her off.

When he fell, the rifle had slipped out of his hands. It was somewhere on the ground now, and he couldn't stop fighting her to find it. The old man was out of commission, at least.

Abel let his arms fall to the side and then balled his right fist and let fly. His punch connected with the side of her head. He heard her make a terrible growling sound, deep in her throat, and her eyes rolled back for a moment.

Her fists slowed down a little, too, so he took the opportunity to punch her again.

She listed to one side, giving him the opportunity to roll out from under her. He caught sight of the rifle and lunged for it on his hands and knees, but then he heard a distinctive *click*. He froze, his hand halfway to the rifle, and looked up.

Cap was sitting against a nearby tree now, his back to it. He had the pistol trained on Abel's head. "You need to back away, son," Cap said. "You've done enough damage tonight."

"I ain't done shit," Abel sneered. It was a lie, but he was justified.

"You killed a man, best I can see." Cap raised his chin and met Abel's blurry gaze.

Abel's eyebrows furrowed. He shook his head. "No, not a chance. I didn't kill that man..." Wait. Was the old guy talking about Rick or the husband, Ethan? Abel didn't know. He clamped his lips shut. His throat was tight. He nodded at Quinn, who was still on the ground, still glaring at him with the heat of hell. "Maybe she did it."

Cap rolled his eyes. His voice was scratchy. "Shut up."

"No way, man. I ain't taking the fall for that." He felt trapped. Beaten. The pistol, aimed directly at his temple, felt like a nail in his skull. His chest hurt.

He would not go back to prison.

He lunged for the old man, landing hard enough to make Cap grunt. They both landed in the snow. The gun flew out of Cap's hand, but Abel didn't see where it went. He needed to find it, secure it, but the old man had more strength than Abel bargained.

Cap pushed back, following Abel over in a heap. The back of Abel's head smacked hard on a branch or a rock or something buried in the snow and the world swam sideways for a minute. He reached up and blindly pushed against the weight on his abdomen, but it wasn't enough. Cap was just pulling back to deliver a jarring blow when Quinn said, "Cap."

Both men looked over at her, and Abel's eyes went wide. She was standing over them with both the rifle and the pistol in her hands. She looked tall and strong, much stronger than she had earlier. Abel had seen a woman look like that before - she had the stance of somebody who didn't give one damn about whether he lived or died.

His wife had that look a couple of times, and it always enraged him, just like it did now. Women were weak, so when one looked like this it was just as if they were lying to him. Quinn Galloway might have a gun in her hand, but she wouldn't pull the trigger. She literally didn't have the balls.

"Cap, get up. It's under control," Quinn said quietly. Her shoulder shook a little, and her voice was breathy and tired.

Cap pushed up off the ground, favoring his leg. Abel started to get up too, but Quinn stepped closer and aimed the gun at his head. "Not you."

Abel looked at Cap. Cap was studying his hand and smiling a little. His knuckles were covered with black.

Blood. Abel felt his face and came away with red fingertips. A cut had opened up along his right jawbone. He winced when he found it.

Only then did he realize how badly his head hurt. He was aching all over, his eyes weren't staying focused, and he thought he was gonna puke if he couldn't get some air. He looked at Quinn, looked at the gun, and got up anyway.

Cap started to say something, but Quinn shook her head. "Would you go get some help?" she asked him.

Abel watched the old man. Cap looked at her and then turned his head to Abel.

Abel expected him to refuse, but he didn't. With an odd light in his eyes, he nodded at Quinn, looked at Abel and turned to hobble toward the ATV parked up the hill a little.

Abel watched him for a moment, then turned back to Quinn.

He would have tackled her right then, but the old man might have another weapon on the machine. She didn't seem to be in a hurry, either, so he was content to wait a few minutes. Then he was going to take away her guns and do what he'd set out to do in the first place - make her give up the goods. After that, well, he'd most likely kill her. She would never be the kind of woman he needed.

She didn't move at all. She just stood there, her knuckles pale on the grip of the pistol, staring at him. She didn't blink or anything. Like a snake, Abel thought. Just like a damned snake.

A short, sharp yelp made him turn his head. The dog came limping out of the trees, moving slow, looking for its master. Quinn saw it too, and a soft smile parted her lips. "Retro," she crooned. "Good boy."

The dog's fur was matted and black with blood. Abel had shot him twice. How was the animal still moving?

He glanced to the spot where Cap had disappeared, then looked back at Quinn. "You're gonna have to put him out of his misery," he said, feeling a small twinge of glee at the thought of hurting her, even with just his words.

She looked at him. "I know."

"He ain't good for nothin' now. Just a mangy, useless mutt."

"I know."

Beyond the edge of the trees, the Gator started up and roared away. "You think the cops are going to get here anytime soon?" he asked.

"Nope."

He pulled his chest up and grinned at her. "You just gonna stand here and try to keep from freezin' till somebody saves you? Stupid bitch."

"Nope." Quinn dropped the rifle on the ground and put her hand on the dog. It nuzzled her hand with its nose and sighed. Good - that would make it easier to disarm her. "Like you said Abel - why try to save a useless, mangy old mutt? I'm going to put him out of his misery."

Abel shook his head. What the hell did she mean?

But then she raised the pistol and he understood. He only heard one shot, the first, but there were three before she stopped, all of them buried in his skull and throat.

Chapter Twenty-Five

Abel, for all his sour hatred and false bravado, fell silently. No screams or groans or any words at all. Quinn watched, amazed, as he toppled into the snow. Blood bloomed on the white, rushing outward, as if to get away from the dying man. The ragged hole in his forehead looked bottomless to Quinn. Part of his throat was torn away, too, but she didn't let her gaze linger there.

When he hadn't moved for a long, long time, she finally tore her eyes away and looked at Retro. "Good boy," she said, reaching for him. "I thought I'd lost you."

She wanted to cry. Needed to, probably. But though her eyes burned, the tears wouldn't come. She knelt down and hugged her dog, ignoring the blood, and they still didn't come.

Retro leaned into her for a while, absorbing her warmth. Eventually, when she didn't move, he dragged himself over to sniff at the dead man.

She would say that she sent Cap away because he was old and hurt. She would say that Abel tried to take her gun. She would say that it was self-defense. Would it work? She didn't know. She didn't know anything about the law when it came to things like this. All she knew was that there was no one to testify otherwise, and that was all that mattered.

Retro whined up at her. She smiled and went to hug him again. His body was warm against hers, but she knew she needed to get him in out of the weather, same as she had done with Cap. "You'll keep my secret, won't you, boy?"

He whined.

She gathered the flashlight and the rifle, put the pistol in the waistband of her jeans, and tried to lift Retro. He was such a big dog, she knew immediately that it was impossible. "You want to stay put, boy? I'll go get the four-wheeler."

She didn't like leaving him here, but she didn't know what else to do. She rubbed his ear and turned away, but he stood, stumbled and tried to follow her.

She opened her mouth to tell him to stay, but then she didn't. The walk back to the house was just going to be a slow one. Together, they started making their way through the woods.

The trip took a good hour, and Quinn remained numb the whole way. She didn't let herself analyze what had just happened, didn't even let herself admit it. There would be time for all that later. Right now, she just wanted to be home. She didn't know what to do about the damage to Retro's side, where he'd been shot. The bleeding had apparently stopped, but by the time they were halfway home it started again. He was tearing at it a little with every step. She cringed when she heard how ragged his breathing was, but she didn't know how to help him besides a few soothing and encouraging words. *Please let him live*, she prayed, harder than she had ever prayed for anything. So hard that her chest burned with it. *Please. I'll do anything.*

When she caught sight of the lights of home, glinting through the trees, she let out a long breath that she didn't know she'd been holding. "Almost there, boy. Just a little bit farther."

Retro huffed at her and kept going, one slow, loping step at a time, his eyes fixed on the house.

Cap was waiting for them in the driveway. Quin was so surprised that she stumbled.

He climbed down and headed their way. He seemed haggard and stooped, as ready to be done with this night as she was.

She looked at the ground when he got to her. "You knew," she said. It wasn't a question.

He fell in beside her, walking just as slow and favoring his damaged leg. "Of course I knew. It was fitting."

They were silent until they got to the house. Cap looked at Ethan and then bent to cover his face. Quinn looked away, helped Retro up the porch steps.

Cap followed her through the half destroyed door, into the house. Retro immediately flopped down into the rug in front of the fireplace. There were only a few small embers left. The room was cold. "You'll be sick later," he said. "When you warm up and think about it. That happens."

She nodded. "OK."

"I want to help with the dog. I'll need some things."

He told her what he wanted and she went through the house - the cold, foreign house - to fetch supplies. Needles, fishing line from Ethan's tackle box in the closet. Aspirin. Rubbing alcohol. A shot of whiskey. A pair of tweezers.

Cap popped an aspirin and gave two to Retro. Then he drained the whiskey, told her to get herself some, and started arranging the rest on the small side table beside Ethan's chair.

Quinn turned away. She didn't want to watch. She busied herself while Cap worked, going out to the barn to find a tarp, heavy and green, and then using the staple gun to attach it over the front door. It cut down on the cold air pouring in. Then she built up the fire in the fireplace again and set to work sweeping up the mess, the wood splinters and the glass. The door and its frame would have to be completely replaced. When she was finished she went back to the living room.

"Help me up," Cap said. "My knees are old."

"Your ankle might be broken, too," she said. "You need to sit."

He did. She brought him another shot of whiskey. "To warm you up," she said, handing it over.

He took it, but this time he simply sipped, his eyes closed, exhaustion deepening the lines on his face.

She knelt down beside Retro, who had borne Cap's work nearly silently, and ran her hand down his flank. "Will he be OK?" she asked.

"I think so. Watch him for a while. You might want to get him to a vet as soon as you can." He chuckled. "I've taken care of cattle, not dogs."

"No -. You probably saved him. Thank you."

"He's a good boy."

"He is," she agreed, and then the tears finally threatened. She held them back. "He's all I've got left, and I almost lost him."

"You didn't."

"Thank you."

This time he just nodded and changed the subject. "You got any pie?"

Her head came up. The absurdity of the question. "What?"

"Pie? Do you have any pie?" He opened his eyes. "That's why I came here. I just wanted pie."

She bit back her laugh, but then let it out. "You came all this way, through a snowstorm...for ...pie?"

"Well, half, anyway."

"I think I've got pie," she said, getting up out of the floor and shaking her head. "I'll get you some."

She didn't believe for a minute that he came out in a snowstorm for a slice of, as it turned out, apple pie. Her best guess was that he wanted her to stop thanking him.

When she came back into the room, it was much warmer. The tarp was doing its job. "Here you go."

He took it with quiet thanks and she went back to Retro. The dog was asleep, looking more peaceful that she thought was possible.

He's with his human," Cap said. He'd been watching them. "That's all that matters to him."

She nodded. "I feel bad for leaving him behind," she said. "I thought he was dead."

"Don't matter now, does it? He ain't. You ain't. Most importantly, I ain't." He grinned.

Chapter Twenty-Six

Q uinn shook the young woman's hand awkwardly and stepped aside to invite her into the cabin. Then she smiled at each of the three children that followed. They didn't smile back. The little girl - Quinn had learned that her name was Angel - simply looked at her shoes and filed in behind her brothers Lyle and Cody. Cute names, cute kids. She closed the brand new front door against the heat of the summer afternoon and sighed.

Patty Fuller was a thin woman who carried an air of despair wherever she went. Quinn didn't know if this was new, or if she'd always been that way. "Please, make yourselves at home," she said, waving toward the sofa. "I'll get us something cool to drink."

Patty's nod was barely there.

Quinn went into the kitchen and got a pitcher of tea from the refrigerator. She had infused it with the juice of fresh peaches, the way Ethan always liked it.

When she carried the pitcher and a set of matching glasses back into the living room, Angel was curled up on her mommy's lap, nearly asleep.

"I don't know how to thank you," Patty Fuller said. "I mean..."

Quinn stopped her by waving a hand. "You need this more than I do."

It was true. In the quiet after the police had come and the commotion had died down, Quinn had discovered a few things. First, she hated the cabin, now that Ethan wasn't here to share it with her. The place was poisoned with terrible, bloody memories, and she wanted nothing to do with it. Second, she learned that she wasn't afraid anymore. She wanted to move back to Atlanta and build something that was hers now. She had already bought a new house in the suburbs, not far from where she and Ethan had lived. Today she was attending to the last bits of business here.

Ethan had forfeited any claim to the rest of her life, and she was still angry about that. The therapist said it was normal, and Quinn had stopped feeling guilty about it. She would forgive him eventually, she supposed, but she wasn't forcing it.

Patty's boys had found the body of their father a week after Ethan died, caught up in brambles along the bank of the river, a half-mile downstream from their house. The boys had been fishing. Quinn had gone to - and paid for - his funeral.

As it turned out, she suddenly had more money than she knew what to do with, and Patty had nearly nothing. Both women had lost so much, Quinn wanted to ease the younger woman's burden. Maybe doing so would serve to ease her own.

The boys were bored already. They pulled out identical phones and started playing games, leaving the adults to talk.

Patty looked more than exhausted now. She looked ready to cry. "I still don't know why you are doing this," she said.

Quinn smiled. Patty, she had learned, came from the kind of background where every gift had a price and every good carried something bad right along behind it. She had fought hard for everything she had, but nearly all of it had been lost the night Abel Welch killed her husband. She had fallen apart, according to Cap, who got his gossip from Sunday morning services at the First Baptist in town.

Not three months after Quinn had buried Ethan, she was attending Cap's funeral. His leg had healed from his night in the woods, but his lungs were never quite right after that. Quinn hung all the blame on Abel Welch for his death, and she didn't feel a bit ashamed to do it. She visited his grave once a week with Mary.

Ethan had been cremated, as he requested in the will she didn't know he had, and so there was no grave for him. She hadn't asked to keep the ashes - she didn't want them. He wasn't there anymore, and she had no use for a guilt shrouded urn.

And there was guilt, along with the sadness and anger. There was plenty of guilt. What had she done to make him think he couldn't come to her? Why hadn't she noticed that something was wrong? Had she missed the signs? Had he tried to tell her and she didn't listen? These questions circled her mind for days at a time, until she realized that she was wallowing and put a stop to it. There were no answers, so dwelling on them only hurt her.

Patty pulled the familiar blue envelope from her glossy black purse and held it in both hands. "I just don't know what to say."

"I don't want you to say anything. I want you to live here, enjoy your home, love your kids, and try to forget." Quinn had told her this a hundred times. "The paperwork is done. This is all yours."

She turned away and dug into her own purse. She pulled out a jangling ring of keys and handed them over. "The four-wheeler," she said pointing. "The tractor. The truck. The barn, and the garage here." She paused, then shoved the set into Patty's cold hands. "I'm sure you'll figure it out."

Patty nodded. "The boys will be so happy."

Quinn glanced at them. "Have you told them yet?"

Patty shook her head. "I wasn't sure..."

"All of my things are gone, so you should be good to go," Quinn said, standing up.

Patty was staring hard at the keys. It took Quinn a moment to realize that she was crying. It took the kids another moment, but when they did, they jumped to attend to her.

"Momma?" Angel said, looking up.

Her tone of voice got the boys' attention. "Hey, Mom?" the older one, Cody, said. "You all right?"

Patty nodded and reached over to squeeze his arm. He noticed the keys.

Quinn gathered her purse to her side and walked to the door, leaving them to their privacy. "Please enjoy it," she said. "It's a wonderful home. I know you'll be happy here." She paused and looked around. "It's just not a good place for me."

Patty nodded, but didn't get up.

Quinn let herself out, walked to her car, and whistled for Retro. He came bounding around the corner of the house. "Come on buddy," she said, opening the rear door of her SUV. He hopped up into the giant carrier that took up the entire back seat. "Let's get out of here."

The day was bright and hot over her head as she backed out of the driveway and turned toward the sun. She never wanted to see winter again.

About Pinwheel Books

Thanks so much for purchasing this book. I hope you enjoyed it! I love to hear what readers think, so if you have time please head over to Amazon to leave a review. You can also email me here.

Check out all of our books at Pinwheel Books[1], or let us send our new release newsletter[2] to your inbox. (We never send email more than once a month, and we don't share. With anyone. Even if they twist our arms. Promise!)

---

1. http://pinwheelbooks.blogspot.com/
2. http://eepurl.com/deYZhn

SCAPEGOAT

ELI GUNN DOESN'T RUN. He didn't run from his broken childhood, he didn't run from his teenaged mistakes, and he didn't run from the cops on that blazing summer night ten years ago. He's fresh out of prison and he may have found a girl who could put up with him and the new quiet life he leads. Things are looking like they might turn out all right.

That is, until the girl disappears without a word or a trace. Faced with a backwoods religious cult that has a tendency to kill off its flock in the name of God...well, Eli's still not running, but now he wants revenge.

---

1. http://www.amazon.com/exec/obidos/ASIN/B01N9EV3A2/litcatstu-20

THE GOOD WIFE

BILL LANDRY IS THE master of his home and land. He's never faced anything that he couldn't crush beneath his wide size twelves or put down with a shot from his rifle. Nobody crosses Bill, including his wife Martha.

Of course, she doesn't have much choice, especially when a hunting accident leaves him home-bound and full of rage. He's becoming more vicious by the day, turning on her and anyone else who ventures too close to their mountain home. She's trapped there with him, and the more deranged he grows, the more she's sure she'll never get out of that valley alive.

---

1. http://www.amazon.com/exec/obidos/ASIN/B00CNXBNI0/litcatstu-20

Made in the USA
Middletown, DE
16 March 2020

86417143R00092